EVALLE
AND
STORM

BOOK 10.5
IN
THE BELADOR SERIES

DIANNA
LOVE

EVALLE AND STORM
The Belador Series, Book 10.5

Copyright © 2019 by Dianna Love

978-1-940651-02-6

Printed in the USA.

Cover Design and Interior Format
© **KILLION**
THE GROUP, INC.

"...an ongoing fantasy series, and definitely not the end, nor is it a cliff hanger. I loved the ending and can't wait for the next book to come out."
~~ Madison Fairbanks, Amazon

"What a ride!!! This series keeps getting better and better."
~~ Gaby, Amazon

ROGUE BELADOR

"When it comes to urban fantasy stories, Dianna Love is a master."
~~ Always Reviewing

"Brava Ms. Love for another fantastic ride."
~~ In My Humble Opinion

"It was worth every day of waiting."
~~ J. Cazares, Amazon

"As always, Dianna Love delivers another sensational story that will blow your mind."
~~ The Reading Café

WITCHLOCK

"Every scene in WITCHLOCK is absolutely spellbinding... This remarkable author repeatedly leaves you wondering if there truly are happenings on earth of which we are not aware."
~~SingleTitles.com

"I LOVE THESE BOOKS! I wait impatiently for every book to come out and have never been disappointed."
~~Elizabeth, Reader

DEMON STORM
"There is so much action in this book I feel like I've burned calories just reading it."
~~D Antonio, Goodreads

"...I have to thank Dianna for keeping this series true to the wonderful world, witty dialogue and compelling characters that I have loved since the first book."
~~Chris, Goodreads

RISE OF THE GRYPHON

"...It's been a very long time since I've felt this passionate about getting the next installment in a series. Even J. K. Rowling's Harry Potter books."
~~Bryonna Nobles, Demons, Dreams and Dragon Wings

"...shocking developments and a whopper of an ending... and I may have exclaimed aloud more than once...Bottom line: I really kind of loved it."
~~Jen, Amazon Top 500 Reviewer

THE CURSE

"The Beladors series is beloved and intricate. It's surprising that such a diverse and incredible world has only three books out."
~~ USA Today, Happy Ever After

"If you're looking for a series with an epic scope and intricate, bold characters, look no further than the Belador series."
~~Bridget, The Romance Reviews

ALTERANT

"There are SO many things in this series that I want to learn more about. As Evalle would say, 'Bring it on.'"
~~Lily, Romance Junkies Reviews

"An incredible heart-jolting roller-coaster ride ... An action-packed adventure with an engrossing story line and characters you will grow to love."
~~ Mother/Gamer/Writer

BLOOD TRINITY

"BLOOD TRINITY is a fantastic start to a new Urban Fantasy series. I am finding it difficult to wait for the next book to find out what happens next in their lives."
~~Diana Trodahl, Fresh Fiction

"BLOOD TRINITY is without a doubt one of the best books I've read this year... a tale that shows just how awesome urban fantasy really can be."
~~ Debbie, CK2s Kwips & Kritiques

EVALLE AND STORM: BELADOR BOOK 10.5

New York Times bestseller Dianna Love's Beladors are back with a special story for Evalle and Storm!

———•———

To bond or not to bond should be a simple question, but nothing is ever easy in the life of this Belador and Skinwalker couple.

Evalle cheated death after Storm and her friends pulled her from a brutal imprisonment in another realm only to now end up unable to shift into her gryphon. Against his better judgment, Storm agrees to hold off on bonding while they travel to Arizona to help his uncle figure out what is behind an unnatural death on the reservation. The more powers Evalle loses, the more she realizes linking to Storm could be lethal. As the investigation takes an unexpected turn, Evalle jumps at a chance to regain her gryphon and powers in an all-or-none gamble, but makes a deadly mistake. Storm has a breakthrough on the unnatural deaths only to realize he's put a target on Evalle's back.

"As always, Dianna Love delivers another sensational story that will blow your mind."
~~ The Reading Café on the Beladors

———•———

Belador books come in e-book, print and audio.

For signed books, book plates and swag, visit
www.DiannaLoveSignedBooks.com

(New books go up for preorder first on this site. You'll be able to order a book signed, personalized and shipped 2+ weeks early – just sign up to be notified about preorders.)

DEDICATION

Thank you to Stacey Krug for always being ready to jump in and help. I appreciate you so much.

PRONUNCIATION GUIDE

Note: A complete guide of unusual names, places and terminology is located on any Belador book page at *www.AuthorDiannaLove.com.*

Adsila – ahd-SEE-lah
Ashaninka – ah shuh NEEN kuh
Betatakin - buh TA TAH kin
Bidziil – BIDE shee-el ("dz" pronounced together as "ds")
Daegan – DAY gan
Evalle – EE vahl (rhymes with hall)
Gad - (rhymes with lad)
Haloke – how – LOKE – ee
Garwyli – gar WHY lee
Imala - EE mah lah
Kai – (rhymes with pie)
Medb – Mave (rhymes with grave)
Nascha - NASH uh
Noirre – NOIR eh (similar to soiree)
Tahoma – tay HOME uh
TÅμr – tower
Tzader – ZAY dur
Yazzle - YAZ ul (rhymes with dazzle)

CHAPTER 1

Navajo reservation near the Grand Canyon in Arizona

B IDZIIL STEPPED FROM THE DARKNESS swallowing miles of empty land in every direction and into the faint light cast by a single bulb outside the lone trailer.

He called out, "Nascha?"

No one appeared at the door. No lights shined inside.

Frustrated, he shouted, *"Nascha!"*

Still nothing.

Everyone came to Bidziil to fix their problems.

Where was someone when he needed help?

Sonny's corpse continuously flashed through Bidziil's mind. Bile rushed up his throat, but he had nothing else to throw up. Tears leaked down his face.

Sonny had been a twenty-two-year-old rising star. No, he'd been so much more, a young man Bidziil would've been proud to call a son.

Bidziil had to find Nascha. He staggered to his left, feeling every one of his fifty-eight years with each heavy step.

Sonny's mangled face demanded he not stop.

"I won't, Sonny," Bidziil promised. He would *not* sleep until he got answers. If Sonny had died naturally or by accident, he could at least understand it, but what he saw tonight defied description.

Once he passed the old trailer and entered the quiet land beyond, he caught a whiff of smoke. He closed the distance to where a lone figure squatted in front of a campfire.

Feeling a surge of energy, he took off again. His last stride brought him to the opposite side of the fire. Forcing his voice to calm, he said, "Nascha."

Burned herbs and singed wood scents filled the air.

Nascha lifted a dark gaze to pin him. Eyes once brown were black pits of anger. Flickering light glowed over wrinkles carved into the sixty-one-year-old weathered face. Nascha's leather vest and a long-sleeved shirt fell loose over his jeans. Still dressing as he had when they were both boys.

Nascha grunted up at him. "You come with questions, but you do not hear truth."

Bidziil's brain would explode if the crotchety old guy started that crap tonight. In a raw voice, he warned, "No riddles. You claim to be a powerful medicine man. We lost Sonny tonight. His face ..." Bidziil's voice fell off. He couldn't get the words out.

Glaring back, Nascha bit out, "I know of Sonny's death."

"Okay, then. Do you know how?" Bidziil held his breath, fearing Nascha would say Sonny had taken drugs or done something equally sickening. Bidziil would need proof before he could accept Sonny hadn't been the squeaky-clean kid he'd watched grow up.

Nascha lifted his lip in disgust. "His death not natural."

"I. Know. That. Tell me something I don't know, dammit."

Nascha moved no muscle, his hard gaze accusing Bidziil of all the wrongs in their clan.

Bidziil didn't blink. He stared right back with determination born of pain so deep it had found a permanent place in his soul.

With a grunt of dismissal, Nascha broke away first.

Words backed up in Bidziil's tight throat. He prided himself on maintaining his calm when others didn't, but his chest vibrated with anger he needed to release. He gave the medicine man one more chance. "What do you think could've caused Sonny to claw his face off? I have someone running a test for drugs—"

"You think Sonny took drugs?" Nascha accused.

"No! I'm just trying to find a reason for something I can't comprehend," Bidziil shouted. He'd mentally searched for any reason, even an unwelcome one, but when the medical examiner suggested the possibility of drugs, Bidziil had lashed out at the poor guy.

With no other explanation, he was being forced to consider the unimaginable.

Nascha crossed his arms and lifted his eyebrows in challenge.

"Dark spirits walk among us."

Bidziil drew in a deep breath, willing himself to stand here until he got information. "Are you saying something like a demon got inside Sonny?" Bidziil believed in the power of men such as his brother, Sani, who should have been their medicine man, and Nascha, but he'd never dealt with a demonic problem.

Nascha made a sound of disgust. "You look for simple answer. Some deaths have many layers."

"That's not helpful at all," Bidziil ground out. He spent time with business people who gave him straight answers and that's all he wanted now.

Nascha crossed his arms. "I am healer, not one who is *supposed* to see problem." His tone of dismissal said as much as him lowering his gaze to the fire did. "Come to me when you know what to heal."

Fisting his fingers to keep from strangling Nascha, Bidziil caught himself. He couldn't lose his control now. Everyone looked to him to be strong, even when his guts felt ripped out.

He stomped back to his sport-utility vehicle a quarter mile away where he'd parked it because he'd dented the rim driving to this trailer the last time.

His next stop would be even more difficult, which was why he'd gone to Nascha first.

Another fifteen minutes down the paved road, Bidziil pulled off to think about his options. He could either call the casino office and wait for an ATV to be delivered or take his chances driving two miles off road to reach the seer's place.

Haloke refused to move to the trailer with running water and utilities Bidziil had provided for her.

She lived in a primitive hogan, a dome-shaped structure covered in mud and positioned near the eastern edge of the Grand Canyon.

Asking for an ATV in the middle of a Friday night would set tongues wagging when Bidziil had to keep this contained until he had a clear indication of how Sonny's death occurred. The minute word got out without an acceptable cause, law enforcement from outside the reservation would flood in.

That never went well.

He'd done everything in his power to protect his clan's sense of independence. One look at Sonny and the US government would get involved. Then this would turn into a media zoo.

Everyone would forget what mattered most—finding the truth of how Sonny died.

Bidziil needed to know for Sonny's benefit and to shield his people from whatever caused this. Bringing in outsiders would shut down any chance at gaining local information.

Sonny would have been the first to offer help if this happened to someone else. He'd been exceptional as a person and an employee.

Bidziil tried not to regret encouraging him to push hard to get ahead. No one knew Sonny's life would be cut short.

Grumbling to himself, Bidziil engaged the four-wheel drive on the Tahoe just to have it ready and pulled off the road, heading across the rough terrain.

Haloke claimed the negative energy and electronics near the rest of the community interfered with her ability to reach beyond this world for answers.

Some rolled their eyes at her claim.

Haloke lacked Nascha's level of power, but she did her best, giving credit to Sani for encouraging her to use her gifts to aid their people. She pinpointed health issues for some as physical or emotional problems, yet missed the mark for others, but not everyone believed in spiritual healing.

Belief was everything.

Bidziil believed in every clan's seers and healers, even Haloke, but no one had a magic wand.

He wished Sani had believed in his plan for the tribe and stayed to help. Instead, Sani took his gifts thousands of miles away to a tribe in South America where he showed them how to preserve their culture while surviving.

Sani died far from his own people.

Bidziil pushed those thoughts aside. He could only deal with one death at a time.

When he reached Haloke's hogan, he found it empty, too.

"Damn." He had much farther to walk this time. With temps in the eighties at night in June, he shed the jacket to his business suit and replaced his wingtips with boots he kept for rough terrain.

Rolling up the sleeves of his white shirt, he began a three-hundred-yard hike to the seer's private spot for visions.

Even with the partial moon offering some light, the glow of

Haloke's fire stood out against a dark backdrop.

Bidziil carried around an extra fifteen pounds, but he also stayed in shape just to deal with the contrary members of their clan who lived off the main roads.

Two to be specific.

By the time he reached the wilting fire where a tendril of smoke swirled from hot coals, his anger had settled into a painful punch in his chest.

Haloke's arms were outstretched and her head bent back. She murmured words that drifted away as they touched the air.

He wanted to show respect for whatever she was doing and not interrupt, but he couldn't stand here all night.

After all, she should have been expecting him.

As he opened his mouth to call out to her, a loud screech from above cut him off. He looked up to see a large bird's silhouette glide across the moon.

Looking over her shoulder, Haloke said, "Come."

What the ...

He tamped down on his anger at being ordered. He'd known Haloke since they were kids when she'd gone by a different name. She'd been bossy as a teen and hadn't changed much over the years. Many called her Bird Woman due to her repairing wings and healing any sick bird.

Regardless of how she'd acquired her name, he would always be her friend for many reasons. One had been how she'd supported him when Sani left.

Bidziil asked, "Do you know why I'm here?"

"Sonny no longer walks with us," she said in a grim voice, more emotion than he'd gotten from Nascha. "He suffered greatly."

Wait ... how did Haloke know?

He understood about Nascha, because the old guy's majik allowed him to see spirits who would have informed him. He'd shared experiences Bidziil considered hair-raising, but the medicine man took it all in stride.

That's why he'd expected to get information from Nascha first.

Haloke had shocked him enough he had to regroup. Taking care how he spoke, he said, "I've kept Sonny's death quiet tonight. Who told you?"

She sighed as if he'd disappointed her with the question. "The eagle brought me news."

Of course.

But if a bird told her what he needed, he'd bring her a year's supply of food for her winged sanctuary.

Two hours had passed since he'd first walked up to Sonny's disfigured body. Grief, anger, and confusion had whittled Bidziil down to this moment where he had nowhere else to go.

He admitted, "I have skilled people going over the body, but we don't even have a starting point of murder, suicide, or natural occurrence."

Nodding solemnly, she remained in one spot, wearing her faded skirt made of two woven rugs and full-sleeved blouse adorned with a beaded necklace. She wore no makeup, but at fifty she still had a striking profile. Silver threads ran through the single black braid hanging over her shoulder.

Pretty, but perpetually sad the past two years.

Losing a child would do that.

Bidziil understood her grief more deeply now.

Looking away into the dark night, Haloke said, "Tell me of this death, Bid. What troubles you about it?"

Those had been the first consoling words he'd heard.

He heaved a deep sigh. "Losing any member of the tribe bothers me, but you know how much I cared for Sonny. The time I spent helping him with studies and the plans we'd made for his future ... he had so much life ahead of him."

She gave him her signature grunt in reply.

· Taking that as a sign to keep going, Bidziil said, "Nothing about this death makes sense. No sign of a murder weapon. There was nothing natural about dying that way, which leaves suicide. The medical examiner said that would only happen if Sonny bled to death from clawing his face, but his body lost little blood." Bidzill scrubbed a hand over his swollen eyes.

"He had claws?" she asked suspiciously.

"No, but his nails were really long." Bidziil shuddered at standing close enough to see those thick fingernails dug into Sonny's skin. "I can't say if they were normal or not, Haloke. Sonny had gloves on most of the time because he worked alongside the laborers."

Bidziil couldn't believe Sonny would not show up grinning and ready for a new day at work tomorrow. The young man's gloves had shown the kind of wear that earned respect from the others.

Focus on his death, not the hole left in my chest. Bidziil cleared his throat. "Sonny was a decent and kind person, a hard working tribal member who didn't deserve to die that way."

He'd mentored Sonny from the age of twelve when the boy's mother died of poor health from living in squalid conditions. Moving him and his father to a better location improved the young man's life, but his father couldn't be cured of alcoholism, a disease fought across many tribal communities.

His father died right after Sonny reached nineteen. Bidziil had been the one standing with Sonny during the burial, just as he had stepped into the paternal role when Sonny needed guidance or to show pride when he won an award at school.

Only last week, Sonny had been excited to show Bidziil a new idea for the warehouse. Seeing that kid happy after all he'd been through had been a proud moment.

Now ... Sonny was dead.

How was that fair? Why him?

Bidziil's vision blurred then cleared.

He glanced over to see Haloke's intense gaze locked on him.

Lifting a trembling hand to wipe his mouth, he said, "I'm trying to figure out what happened. That kid didn't do drugs. I have nothing, nowhere to look."

She shook her head slowly, agreeing.

"Nascha says—"

Haloke hissed at hearing the medicine man's name.

He ground his back teeth, tired and short on patience, then plowed ahead. "Nascha says dark spirits walk among us."

She narrowed her eyes in sullen silence.

Squeezing words from a cactus had to be easier. "What about you, Haloke? Why do you think Sonny did that?"

She spoke with the authority of schooling a child. "You said he clawed his own face off. I do not see how he would do that even with a gun pointed at his head."

Bidziil had already come to the same conclusion. He'd gone to Nascha for spiritual help and walked away with nothing.

Now he had to ask Haloke to go one step further.

"What do you want from me, Bid?" she asked in a taut voice that brought him up short.

Maybe she sensed his hesitation to ask a new question, but he sucked up his courage and got to it.

"Would you reach out to the spirits and find an answer or even a clue for how Sonny died? I'm desperate to figure this out using our people. I don't want to bring in outsiders unless I have no other option."

She drew up straight and stabbed a withering look at him.

He held firm during her silent wrath.

She ordered, "You must *not* bring in strangers. Outsiders will point fingers at our people for fast solutions. That will not deliver justice."

"Agreed, but I still need help." He waited for her decision.

Staring up at the sky, Haloke muttered too softly for him to hear her words clearly. When she finally lowered her head and faced him, she said, "I will ask the Holy People about this death, but Sonny's wind could not have been in balance for this to have happened. To ask about such a death carries risk. They may show mercy and give aid, or they may refuse to respond."

She paused then added, "Or they could choose to take another action."

Even as an adult, he shuddered at contacting those spirits. He'd grown up hearing how the Holy People, sometimes called the Holy Wind, could play nice ... or not.

"Are you in danger if you do this, Haloke?"

The hint of a smile lifted one corner of her lips, but it disappeared just as quickly. "They have no quarrel with me."

Did that mean the Holy People might have a bone to pick with Bidziil? Or Sonny?

She angled her head at him in question.

He said, "I understand your warning. Please, find out what you can."

She ordered, "Move back twenty steps."

Once he reached the distance she'd indicated to allow her a private area, she began singing in their native tongue.

Bidziil caught some words and phrases, but to his detriment he'd become rusty. No one in his inner circle spoke it often, but he should know his tribe's language.

The seer tossed invisible crystals into the fire, sparking tiny bursts of light.

He stood there for a half hour, maybe more, but he couldn't come asking for help and disrespect her by leaving before she spoke to him. To be honest, he had no idea where else to turn at this point without allowing an autopsy.

Authorizing that would result in an uproar.

His people believed the spirit had to be allowed to leave the body naturally four days after death. He might not believe as deeply as he should, but he did hold with not cutting a body open and trapping a spirit. He couldn't leave Sonny's locked in that grotesque body.

Haloke quieted, drawing his attention. He started to move forward, then stopped.

When another long minute had passed, she lifted a hand in his direction, waving him over.

He hurried back, noting the sweat pouring from her face. Standing over even a small fire in this warm temperature had to be tough.

"What did you find out, Haloke?"

The gaze she turned on him was swollen and red as if she'd been bawling the whole time, but she hadn't so much as sniffled. She spoke in a hoarse voice. "The Holy People are not happy with our clan. They will not share how Sonny died."

Bidziil slapped his head. "Another dead end."

"No. There is a path to the truth."

His heart clutched. "Are they willing to give us clues?"

She frowned. "They are not servants to do your bidding."

"That's not what I meant."

Lifting a hand to silence him, she said, "Did Nascha give you answers?"

"No."

"Did he send you to me?"

"*Nooo*," he said, drawing out the word to indicate he did *not* want to waste time on their conflict, which had been ongoing for years.

"Humph." She lifted her chin. "The Holy People sent a message. They advise that one of our blood will bring justice."

Screw it. Bidziil would endure Haloke's criticism of Nascha with no complaint if he left with the name of someone who could help him solve Sonny's death.

Give Sonny a burial he deserved.

Bidziil swallowed at the thought.

Using his most respectful voice, he changed his approach for information. "Thank you, Haloke. Did the spirits offer anything more specific?"

She closed her eyes, but her lids twitched with movement. "Sonny did not take his life, not of his own doing. They warn of more deaths until a wrong is made right."

"*More* deaths?" Bidziil asked, appalled.

Ignoring his outburst, Haloke continued speaking as if she'd fallen into a trance. "The deaths will not end until the old one's child comes to this land." She hesitated and frowned, then continued slowly as if confused. "The Holy People say this child is of your blood. He will bring balance back where the wind is no longer at peace."

Haloke opened her eyes and started shaking her head. "That is not possible. *Old one's child ... of your blood.*" She looked sharply at Bidziil. "That can only be Sani, but he is dead. He had a son?"

Bidziil's breath caught at what she said. He quickly explained, "You're talking about Storm, Sani's only child." Bidziil cut off his next thought before he said too much.

Storm had been born a Skinwalker in South America, something Bidziil's people considered a demon.

Bidziil had met him once.

Storm would not come and Bidziil would not ask him.

If the Holy People thought Storm could solve how Sonny died, then why couldn't Nascha and Haloke work together to do the same?

Haloke gasped. "You *know* of his son?" Then she pushed past her surprise and demanded, "You must bring him here."

"I'll be honest with you," Bidziil said. "Storm does not want to get involved. Don't ask me how I know, but I do."

The smooth skin of her forehead scrunched in disbelief. "After Sani abandoned us, you would protect his son and not your people?"

Bidziil's gut twisted at that accusation, but he stated in a firm voice, "I will do all in my power to protect them *and* Storm, as he is my brother's child. But expecting him to come out here is a wasted phone call."

She stood over the fire, staring down into it and speaking in a dead tone. "You may not have a choice, Bid."

"Why?"

"I warned you about asking the Holy People for anything. Sani's son can refuse them. That does not mean they will accept no from him."

CHAPTER 2

In the Treoir Realm hidden above the Irish Sea

STANDING ON THE WIDE LANDING at the top step to the entrance of Treoir Castle allowed Storm a clear view of his mate as she walked away from him.

The emotional distance between them felt wider than an ocean. His mind warred with his empathic ability, arguing that he should stop wasting time and bond with Evalle.

She needed him.

His heart still hammered fast.

His jaguar pushed him to take their mate somewhere safe where nothing and no one would ever hurt her again.

The resident druid, Garwyli, knew Evalle well. He'd cautioned Storm to not suffocate her. The druid claimed now that he and Storm had done their part, Evalle had to heal from the inside out. He believed none of them could bring her gryphon back.

Evalle had to do it on her own.

Storm couldn't agree. Garwyli meant well, but Evalle would benefit from Storm's power and healing once they bonded.

Evalle crossed the lush open field and disappeared into the woods.

Go or stay? Storm waged that silent battle in his mind. He wouldn't allow anyone, even Garwyli, to keep him from protecting his mate, but she was in no danger here, right?

Still, standing firm to give her room to find her way tore at his insides.

"How's she doing, Storm?" Adrianna asked.

"Shit!" He jerked at being surprised. With his Skinwalker

senses, few people managed to approach him unnoticed.

The witch's eyebrows shot up. "What'd I do?"

"I didn't hear or sense you approaching," he admitted. "That doesn't happen often to me." Like never.

She chuckled. "I'm insulted. You think I can't sneak up on someone?"

He smiled in spite of being caught off guard. "I would never underestimate you or Witchlock," he quipped, noting the ancient power she possessed. "But you've said you don't want to use that majik here, which means I wasn't paying attention." His gaze shot back to the woods.

How long had Evalle been gone?

Adrianna's voice turned consoling. "I saw Evalle walk into the forest. Is that what has you jumpy?"

Storm acknowledged the truth. "I'm having a hard time the minute she's out of my sight."

"Everyone here who went with us to save her can sympathize, but she's safe on Treoir."

He'd been telling himself that for days. It wasn't helping.

Adrianna asked, "How *is* she doing?"

Unfolding his arms, he hooked his thumbs in the front pockets of his jeans. "I'm not sure I can give an honest answer to that question."

"Why? Evalle claims your empathic gift is pretty phenomenal compared to anyone else, especially hers."

"Oh, I'm picking up plenty from her and that's the problem," he grumbled. "It's as if her emotions are frenetic today. Sometimes it feels like I'm getting two conflicting messages at the same time."

Adrianna stepped forward and turned to him with genuine concern on her face. Her normal attire was that of a petite fashionista, but today she'd dressed down in jeans and a red button shirt with her blond hair twisted into some type of bun. A pretty woman, Adrianna could go bald and leave tongues dragging behind her.

All but Storm's.

He appreciated her more for the friendship that had grown between the witch and his mate.

Adrianna rarely showed emotions in public or touched others, but she gently clasped Storm's arm for just a moment. "I don't understand. Evalle's emotions feel like what?"

"Like there is so much going on with her it could be coming from multiple people. No one should have that many conflicting emotions at one time." He caught himself and quickly added, "Please don't share that, Adrianna, because it won't help for everyone to think she's becoming schizophrenic or ... hell, I don't know what word would describe it."

"Of course, I won't," she assured him. "If she were human, what you describe sounds almost along the lines of a dissociative personality disorder."

Two guards walked out of the castle, laughing at some joke.

Storm clamped his mouth shut and backed up a step. He rolled his shoulders.

Talking about Evalle as if she were some psychotic basket case boiled his blood. He should've kept that to himself. His jaguar growled, ready to defend Evalle.

"Storm, uh, calm down, okay?" the witch whispered.

He glanced down at Adrianna, who stood just two inches over five feet tall. Energy pulsed through his gaze.

Why was she staring at him as if his head was on backwards? "What, Adrianna?" His question came out on a growl.

Keeping her voice discreet, she looked around first then said, "I feel energy pouring off you and your eyes turned red for a moment."

He yanked his emotions under control and checked their surroundings, too.

Belador guards walked in a group on the far left. Gryphons flew overhead, swooping in and out of the clouds and gutting him with another reminder of what Evalle had lost.

He would find a way to give her back her gryphon.

His attention snapped back to the tree line. Should he give her more time? Back and forth, he fought to sit tight and be patient or check that she was safe every damn minute of the day.

Adrianna tapped him on the shoulder and suggested, "Let's walk."

With a last cursory glance to be sure no one stood close enough to hear them, he said, "Right behind you."

Storm waited until he and Adrianna were far enough from any of the others to say, "It's killing me to watch Evalle struggle just to get her life back. She's not happy Daegan isn't ready to send her back to Atlanta to join the Belador teams, but neither am I. She freaking died." He shook his head in wonder at those words and having watched her stop breathing. "I'm just happy she's alive."

"I've been through my own trials with someone close, so you know I understand. But I also can see where Evalle's anxious to get back to what her life was before the kidnapping."

Adrianna did understand. She never wanted Witchlock, but she'd taken it to free her twin sister who had been trapped by a crazy witch who had turned her sister's body into a shell. The connection between the twins had to have been brutal with Adrianna hearing her sister in her head, screaming in agony for months until she could free her.

The witch cocked an eyebrow. "What's your plan? I know you have one and I'm willing to help any way I can. In fact, I talked to Garwyli this morning."

Storm held back a scoff. She gave him more credit than he gave himself. "I haven't talked to the druid in two days. What'd he tell you?"

She tilted her head. "Garwyli warned me not to interfere. He believes we can't fix Evalle."

"He told me that too, but he's wrong," Storm snarled.

She held up a hand then pointed at herself. "Messenger." As in don't take her head off for just sharing what she knew.

"Sorry." He seemed to be saying that a lot. Evalle wouldn't allow him to say that word to her right now. She claimed no one was at fault for something none of them could have seen coming.

Maybe. But he could have been better prepared.

If he'd bonded her to him before she'd been kidnapped, he'd have found her quicker.

"Storm, you still with me?" Adrianna asked as she stopped.

Shit. Shifting his gaze from where he kept watching for Evalle to the witch, he muttered, "I'm back."

Adrianna continued in the same steady voice. "I also asked Garwyli if Evalle would do better here or back in Atlanta where she probably feels more at home."

"What'd he say about that?" Storm had thought the same thing, but he assumed Evalle would continue healing faster in Treoir where her Belador power got a boost.

He'd brought Evalle's two-foot-tall gargoyle, Feenix, to Treoir Castle along with her clothes to give her some sense of home. She'd been thrilled to watch Feenix play outside with no worries of discovery for the first time since she'd rescued him from a sadistic mage.

Feenix and Evalle had a bond as close as any mother and child.

That gargoyle had wanted no part of Storm nor would he share Evalle for the longest time, but Storm had been just as determined to stay.

Of all the ways Storm had tried to develop a relationship with that possessive little gargoyle, finding Evalle in another realm and bringing her home had earned Storm a hug and being called, "Mine."

In Feenix's world, that was the highest honor given to someone other than Evalle.

Lifting her eyes to gryphons flying high in the sky, Adrianna muttered, "Evalle needs her gryphon back." Looking to Storm, she said, "Sorry, it's not like we don't all want that. Garwyli said there was no way to know for sure if staying here or going to Atlanta would be better for Evalle without giving her the chance to find out. He firmly believes we need to allow her space to figure some things out on her own."

Storm grumbled, "I'm trying, dammit."

"I know," Adrianna said on a sigh. "I also know how hard it is for you. I want to spin up Witchlock and fix whatever ails her, and I would, but I have no idea how that would turn out. Right now, Garwyli is the only one of us not hovering. He may have a point."

"Maybe I should take her to Atlanta." Storm couldn't say that with conviction. What about the preternatural threats waiting in the human world? "I'm torn. I want her home, but Evalle's not in danger here."

"I get that, but being in Treoir is like going on vacation," Adrianna pointed out. "At some point, everyone wants to go home. People heal better in their own environment in most cases." The witch snapped her fingers. "Getting back to what I was saying, Daegan came in on the end of my conversation with Garwyli and argued that Evalle was *not* ready to battle anyone."

Storm had no quarrel with that opinion. He asked, "Did that change Garwyli's mind?"

"No. He said Evalle didn't have to go out looking for trouble. Daegan stomped around complaining he did not want her in danger at all, then Garwyli reminded the dragon you wouldn't let anyone dangerous get near her."

"Damn right," Storm confirmed.

Adrianna smiled at him and said, "Garwyli argued he'd seen Evalle in training battles this week where she could be hurt just as easily. Daegan said he'd order the guards to stay away from her. Garwyli threw his hands up and made it clear everyone needed to stop trying to run her life. That shut Daegan up for a second."

Well, damn. Storm grabbed his head. "Did the druid say *I* was trying to run her life?"

"No, don't take that personally, Storm. Garwyli did say if we keep asking if she's getting better and interfering when she tests her body, she's never going to realize she can fall and get up again." Adrianna took a moment and gentled her words. "He has a point. Evalle's a warrior. She might need to fail so she remembers how to dust her pants off and continue on."

Storm crossed his arms. "I can't argue with that."

The witch lifted her shoulders. "Exactly. Even Daegan thought on that a minute and finally agreed. Then he announced he had full faith in you keeping her safe and he'd teleport you two to Atlanta right away if you agreed."

Daegan's concern for Evalle didn't surprise Storm because the dragon leader of the Beladors had shown he put his followers first time and again. Storm blew out a breath of frustration. "Garwyli made a valid point, but Daegan hasn't said a word to me about teleporting."

Adrianna rolled her eyes. "That's because Brina heard them talking about taking Evalle somewhere else and hurried in, pitching a fit. That brought Tzader storming in and demanding to know who had upset Brina so close to having the twins."

Storm found his smile. "Drama just like in the human world."

She chuckled. "I called up a tiny spell to keep their attention away from me and tiptoed out as they argued."

"*None* of them saw you leave?" Storm asked, seriously amazed.

"Oh, yes. Just before I reached the door, I caught Garwyli sneaking a look my way with a smile. He winked. Hard to slip anything past that one. I think the old druid enjoys getting them all cranked up."

Storm smiled. "I think you're right. Garwyli told me the castle hadn't felt this alive for centuries."

Squawking erupted in the air from the gryphons flying above him. Storm cut his gaze up, dismissed the ruckus then glanced over to the woods, hoping to see Evalle emerge.

Hoyt entered the forest carrying a sword.

What the hell was that Belador up to?

CHAPTER 3

THE MINUTE EVALLE ENTERED THE tree line, hiding her
from all eyes around the castle, she took off at a sprint.

She had to get out of this realm today.

That wouldn't happen if she couldn't prove herself right now.
Her body wouldn't give her any more time.

Pumping her arms flicked her right bicep into view. The jagged
black lines that appeared like inked veins this morning were still
there.

What the hell did that mean?

Knocking branches aside, she kept moving and listened for
Hoyt. She couldn't hear a sound following her.

That meant nothing.

The head of the Belador castle guards might have six inches on
her five-foot-ten height and outweigh her by fifty pounds, but he
could move all that with stealth.

Just like Storm, who shifted into a black jaguar.

She hadn't looked back before leaving Storm's sight. Was he
still talking to Adrianna?

Or was her Skinwalker mate proving he could give her space?

Sweat drizzled down the side of her face even though the
temperature stayed at a comfortable seventy degrees. The Treoirs
controlled the weather and everything else here. Good thing. Real
sunlight would fry her body.

She hunted for a place far enough from the castle to make
a stand and found it when she broke into a clearing. A pile of
boulders three times her height blocked an exit on the other side.

Breathing like a lathered racehorse, she swung around to wait
for Hoyt.

Bad sign being this winded.

Her Belador powers normally got a burst of extra juice in this realm.

Her pulse throbbed from anxiety more than exertion. She'd wanted to be wrong about the lack of power she could feel when she got up this morning, but being out of breath?

Yep, it sucked to be right.

She hadn't felt her gryphon since escaping the Abandinu realm and now her Belador powers were weakening.

Really? *What the hell, Universe?*

She clenched her eyes against the burn of tears. No fucking way was she giving in to the ache of losing her majestic beast, but damn it all. She had a dead spot in her chest where she should feel the buzz of her gryphon's energy.

Garwyli and Storm, the two most powerful healers she knew of, had done all they could.

She was on her own now. Finding a way to fix her body meant getting out of Treoir. Going a route that might not suit everyone here, including Storm.

Her poor mate had been through enough.

She wanted to go home to be with him most of all.

Time for her to up her game. First step would be battling Hoyt to the finish without giving in. He stood between her and convincing their dragon king to teleport her back to Atlanta where she could rejoin the Belador teams.

Being a warrior was all she knew. They could not take that from her. Not without a fight.

Based on testing her powers this morning, she might lose half in another day.

Hoyt attacked from above.

She lunged to the side, rolled forward and came up on her feet. Had she not heard the air rush past his body, she'd have been standing right where he landed.

"I request a Belador sword," she put to the realm. Bam, it appeared vertically right in front of her. With a quick thanks, she grasped the hilt with both hands.

Hoyt straightened from where he'd landed on bent knees.

One look at that brute and his nickname as the War Machine made sense.

He whipped his sword around, warming up his wrists. "You should have waited three more days as we originally agreed."

She mirrored his moves as he began sidestepping in a circle. When on the short end of the power stick, Evalle defaulted to her mouth. "You feeling puny today, Hoyt? I'll take it easy on you."

"You do that, Evalle, while I show you why you are not ready to do this."

To prove him wrong, she had to stay upright the allotted time of thirty minutes, which had technically started.

Hoyt had set the time limit.

She'd groaned internally but had given him the thumbs-up.

Stupid thumbs didn't know any better.

He made the first move, striking hard. She met his hit and it was on. Hoyt sure as hell wasn't on the Coddle Evalle train, like the others.

Metal on metal clashed. It might be due to adrenaline, but she had a surge of excitement when she bested him with her next hit.

Hoyt stumbled, then twisted his body back into position fast, too fast. He brought his sword around in a horizontal arc that slammed her sword, sending her backwards.

He'd done that from his weak side.

Who was she kidding?

He had no weakness.

She felt that contact hammer all the way through her body. In contrast to his size, Hoyt's footwork would impress a ballet prima donna.

Ten minutes in, her sword strikes began to lose punch. She couldn't do this for another twenty minutes against that wall of muscle.

She'd been taught there was only one rule of battle.

To win.

Hoyt took his time coming in for another attack. That screamed confidence. He wouldn't kill her, at least not intentionally. But she'd told him to battle her as if she threatened the life of Brina, their queen whose very existence in the Treoir realm fueled Belador power.

That challenge might go down as a bad life decision.

In response, Hoyt appeared prepared to chop her into pieces and deliver them to Brina as evidence of performing his duty.

Evalle barely sidestepped a powerful hit and sprinted across the clearing. Flipping her sword back and forth, she kept her wrists and arms loose.

If she had plenty of power, she'd still feel warmed up and ready.

Screw this. Forcing energy into her legs, she whipped to the left and spun to hit Hoyt with a scissor kick.

Nailed it.

But Hoyt barely sweated, dammit.

The halter top, one-piece black outfit she wore for sword training had soaked all the way through with perspiration.

He'd stated he would not use kinetics to even out their size difference.

She'd considered arguing, but simply decided to avoid using hers if possible.

That decision fell in the first minute.

Pulling in deep gulps of air, she attacked with a renewed vigor, watching for an opening to toss him off his feet.

Flipping a loaded dump truck over would be easier.

He'd been battling at a steady level of strength then caught her off guard when he struck with a more powerful blow. His sword slammed into hers, knocking her weapon flying.

Damn. Damn. *Damn!*

She didn't hesitate to move, rushing right then left, leaping on boulders and spinning away. Not bad reflexes. Moments like this encouraged her she could win the war with her body.

She sent a slap of kinetics at Hoyt's boots, her only hope for slowing him down.

He continued forward with a kick, as if flipping away an irritation.

Crap. She had seconds before he would be on her. Looking up, she kinetically flipped a branch down, whacking him across the back of the head.

He went flying face first and sprawled on the ground.

Cheap trick, but he'd expect her to use anything she could get her hands on in a battle when back in Atlanta.

Letting out a loud growl that would give a grizzly pause, Hoyt pushed up quickly to his knees.

He sent her a glare she'd have nightmares over.

Oh, boy.

Fighting a Hoyt intent on doing his duty was one thing. Going up against a pissed-off Hoyt ranked as suicidal.

Worry about that later.

Every second counted right now. She only had to stay in the fight another sixteen minutes to prove she could take on an adversary and walk away.

Her heart pounded faster than a hamster on crack.

Using her kinetics, she called her fallen sword to her. Or tried to ... it remained on the ground ignoring her.

She tried asking the realm for a new sword, which any Belador could do here.

The faint image of a sword wavered into view vertically in front of her then vanished before fully forming.

Now on his feet, Hoyt's dark gaze offered no mercy.

Hmm. She *had* asked to prove herself.

If she survived this, she'd prove insanity came with grit.

Pushing energy into her legs, Evalle took off running. Not an impressive battle move, but it was that or lift her hands in surrender.

No fucking way.

Don't lose sight of the goal, she silently repeated to herself. A tree had helped her moments ago. She slapped kinetic hits over her shoulder at branches above Hoyt to distract him.

He slashed two-inch thick limbs that rained down on him.

Whatever.

Not much of a distraction, but it gave her an opening to put some distance between them. She leaped over bushes and hit the ground hard.

Pain shot up her legs. That shouldn't happen. She rushed on in full stride.

Hoyt's footsteps pounded behind her.

Too fast.

Too close.

Sweat stung her eyes and dampened her clenched fists. Her heart banged her chest wall so hard she expected bruising. Every breath dragged into her lungs came back out on a ragged exhale.

Running would not save her.

Twelve minutes.

She zigzagged, ready to panic until she found a decent place to take a stand. Most of the underbrush grew close to the ground and the leaf canopy opened for a wide shot of the blue sky.

If she had one more burst of energy, one more push of kinetics, one more time to call up a sword, then she still had a chance of success.

If not ...

Never waste time thinking on failure.

Hoyt's footsteps slowed as he neared where she waited. He approached with caution.

Wise man. She'd gotten the best of him one time.

Just once.

She doubted many did that and walked away with their limbs intact.

"Please, just one more sword," she begged the realm.

Hallelujah, one appeared in front of her. A masterpiece made of brilliant silver metal stronger than steel and with a Belador triquetra formed in the hilt.

Eight minutes. *Come on, body,* she begged silently. *You can do this a little longer.*

Gripping the weapon, she grimaced at the numbness bleeding into her fingers.

Her gaze jumped to the jagged black line on her arm that grew another inch.

She'd been declared free of the nasty majik a mage had shoved into her body in the other realm. The dark side of her blood from the Medb, enemies of Beladors, responded to the Noirre majik that bunch wielded. But he'd also cast a spell when he pushed the majik inside her, claiming the Noirre would attack her body if anyone teleported her from Abandinu's realm.

He'd been proven correct.

She'd died upon leaving.

Her friends had pulled off the impossible by bringing her back to life and healing her.

Could residual Noirre majik be leaking from her body?

Was that the reason the black lines appeared?

Hoyt used the tip of his razor-sharp weapon to move a branch aside then peered into the opening.

She clenched the grip, lifting her sword. This would be her last chance. She dug deep for everything she could muster. Visions of being back in Atlanta with Storm, loving and laughing, rolled past her eyes. Living free to fight alongside her Belador teammates.

Freedom.

She'd fought too long and hard to give up the life she'd earned.

Hoyt's distrustful eyes took in everything from her to nearby trees to the sky above before returning fully to her again. His naked chest barely expanded with each inhale, not the least bit winded. Jeans covered thick thighs inherited along with other rugged features from Nordics somewhere in his bloodline.

"You may think you have little time left," Hoyt said in his baritone voice. He shook his head. "Six minutes will pass as slowly as an hour with every strike this time. I failed to give this match the respect I should have. That won't happen again."

She would be insulted at his admission if not for the fact he'd been doing her a favor, though unintentionally.

But he'd just informed her the gloves were off.

If that warning had been said to undermine her confidence, point to him.

Even so, she would not allow her mind to beat her.

She nodded. "Bring it."

If only those words had come out with a punch of arrogance instead of on a raspy wheeze.

Finally convinced no trap waited for him, Hoyt entered on deft bare feet.

He could've followed her silently. No, he'd wanted her to hear his footsteps as he closed in, for her to feel like a prey run to ground.

She'd have done the same with an adversary.

They might both be Beladors, but she'd made the stakes clear today and he had a duty to give Daegan an honest assessment. She liked Hoyt and would not hold anything against him, but neither would she let her guard down either.

Lifting an eyebrow, he asked, "Ready to admit defeat?"

He could have said something else to chip away at her determination.

Anything but claiming a victory he had not earned.

Instead of answering, she raced forward on attack, slashing her sword to meet his. The constant whack of metal rang out. She normally wouldn't blast forward to battle but executing the unexpected offered her only advantage if she hoped to kill six more minutes.

With Hoyt's first strike this time, his powerful hit bent her knees.

She forced them back straight.

Again and again, she struck to push him off track, to the side, anywhere that prevented standing still.

He gave no ground, efficient and ferocious. He drove her back with each blow no matter which direction she moved the fight.

Damn him, he'd been right. Minutes took forever to pass.

There couldn't be more than three left.

No time to look at her watch.

She called up whatever energy she had left and blinked away the sweat stinging her eyes.

Muscles in Hoyt's jaw bulged with determination. He seemed to get stronger the longer he battled.

She'd experienced that in the past.

But now? Her arms quivered with spent muscles. The energy she called up trickled into her chest, making no effort to flood her limbs.

She couldn't withstand another two minutes.

That left one choice. She made a dangerous move to throw him out of sync and swing her sword up to attack. He'd have to pull back or be cut.

Solid plan.

With the focus of a cobra ready to strike, Hoyt anticipated her move and reacted with precision. He slashed his sword across and down to meet hers.

Her idea should have worked.

Would have, but her arms couldn't follow through. Her sword swung off track and totally missed connecting with his.

Hoyt's eyes flared in surprise.

And her mind screamed, *Nooo!*

CHAPTER 4

E VALLE FLINCHED AT HOYT'S HUGE sword driving at her. A black flash of fury knocked her aside.

Not in time.

The sharp tip slashed a deep cut across her upper arm.

She hissed in pain, grabbing her right arm and rolling on her stomach. Never stay down. She'd sit up just as soon as the world stopped spinning.

A jaguar roared, shaking the ground with his fury.

Clamping her teeth shut to keep from moaning—or throwing up—she shouted, *"Don't, Storm!"*

Twisting to her knees and looking up, she found the jaguar standing between her and Hoyt, who stood very still.

The Belador's gaze jumped between her and Storm. Where Hoyt never showed doubt he could best Evalle, his expression displayed serious respect for Storm's jaguar.

"Storm," she gritted out.

His jaguar head swung to her with glowing yellow eyes. A deep rumble vibrated his chest that threatened Hoyt would bleed for hurting her.

Storm had warned her his jaguar also claimed her as mate and had almost taken over his body when she turned up missing in Atlanta.

Hoyt said, "I'm sorry, Evalle—"

"Not your fault, Hoyt. Give me a minute. Please."

Storm's jaguar snarled at the guard.

"Storm." Her softly spoken word drew him to her quicker than a shout.

That feral gaze swung back to her. Muscles bunched in his jaguar's shoulders and black hair tufted behind his neck.

Was she speaking to her mate or his animal?

The massive jaguar heaved several hard breaths, expanding his chest each time. Then he lowered his head and moved forward to put his big chin lightly on her left shoulder.

He inhaled deeply.

That was her mate reassuring himself she was fine.

Now that Storm realized she wasn't in mortal danger, Evalle said, "Hoyt did exactly what I asked of him."

A deep growl rumbled.

She added, "If you want to be mad, be mad at me. I made a mistake. Hoyt did his best to avoid cutting me at all." Saying more pushed the limits of her ability to sound calm. Warm blood continued to ooze between her fingers, filling the air with a coppery scent. The wound hurt bone deep, but she could have lost the limb.

Shifting his black head to her right side, the jaguar lowered his nose to where her skin had been slashed. As if the wound wouldn't upset him enough, thin black lines continued to spread down her bicep.

In a flash of energy, Storm shifted back to his human form, naked as the day he'd been born. Not that he gave a flip. What man would who walked around in a toned body wrapped with bands of muscle? Plus, Storm lacked the ability to care what anyone thought of him.

Anyone other than her, and she loved every inch of that man, especially naked.

Storm reached down to lift her to her feet. Every move hurt, but she held onto her stoic warrior face.

Failing today had taken a toll on her heart.

She would not fold in front of him or Hoyt.

The Belador guard had given her the chance she'd asked for and she wouldn't fault him for doing his duty when he reported the outcome to Daegan.

Storm's rich brown eyes no longer glowed yellow. His gaze swept from her face to her arm with a frown.

She got ahead of the next problem by saying, "We'll talk about the lines. I think I know what might be going on."

With a look of resignation in place, he rested his palms lightly on her shoulders. On his next breath, he whispered tribal words she'd heard before when he'd healed her in the past. The ones he currently spoke came from his Ashaninka tribe in South America, but he had a few Navajo ones as well, which he'd learned from his father.

She couldn't translate what he said, but she recognized the different cadence between the languages.

Her wound closed, and the pain eased.

The black lines remained.

Hoyt cleared his throat, probably feeling as if he imposed on their moment with Storm standing there naked or maybe he'd had enough of this outing.

Storm looked past Evalle to the warrior. "Sorry, Hoyt."

"No problem."

Evalle backed out of Storm's touch. "Give me a minute, please? I'll meet you at the castle. It's not far. Okay?"

He said nothing, probably already forming his argument, so she added, "I promise I will come straight there and avoid any chance of getting hurt. Again."

She smiled to show him she did understand.

For the last few days, she'd been asking for time to work some things out on her own and he'd given it to her.

He'd reached the end of his patience.

Releasing a pent-up breath that came out on a long exhale, Storm muttered, "Okay." He cupped her face and kissed her. Not a crazy wild kiss, but one that told her how much he still hurt for her. Storm had brought love into her world where she'd had nothing. No one could match his patience, but she wanted to be a partner in their relationship.

Not a constant liability.

When he ended the kiss, he touched his forehead to hers and gave a gentle warning. "I'll wait five minutes once I get to the castle."

Any other time, she'd mouth off with some wiseass reply about not living on anyone's timeframe. Instead, she lifted up and kissed his lips.

Her words came out husky. "Thank you."

He smiled at the sound, bumped a quick peck to her forehead and turned for the castle. Ripped muscle moved across his back. He moved with the grace of his big cat on those powerful legs.

That was all hers.

Annnd Hoyt was still behind her while she ogled her sexy mate.

Letting her sore arm drop to hang straight and give the impression it didn't throb, she walked over to the guard. "Thanks for doing this today. I appreciate the respect you gave my request. Sorry I didn't move fast enough. We both know I should have been cut far worse if not for your incredible reflexes. I clearly haven't recovered from ... well, you know."

For such a large man, Hoyt had a temperate voice when he wasn't hell-bent to kill an opponent. "You're welcome. I'm glad I didn't injure you beyond repair." He paused and shook his head at some thought. "You're doing damn good for having died and come back to life, Evalle. Don't forget that and how much everyone respects you as a warrior. Give yourself a chance to heal and we'll try this again. Okay?"

"Thanks." She allowed her reply to sound as if she agreed, but she didn't.

Hoyt would understand if he knew more, but she had yet to tell Storm what she kept inside.

Speaking of her overprotective mate, she had to face him next.

Turning to head for the castle, she glanced back at the spot where she'd left Hoyt standing, which was now empty. He hadn't teleported since Beladors generally did not posses that ability. He'd vanished silently by tapping into his Belador power.

One of the Alterant-gryphons, like her, had the ability to teleport but it hadn't been a natural gift. Tristan gained it from a wicked concoction he'd drank while imprisoned in a jungle.

Correction. Not like her.

She could no longer claim being a gryphon, maybe not even an Alterant.

Of all the things she'd suffered, losing her gryphon hurt beyond description. She wanted an enemy to stomp to the ground, but those responsible were dead.

The old druid, Garwyli, kept telling her to have faith, that she would have to believe in herself again to recover fully.

She believed an hour ago.

Hard to right now.

She swallowed. Garwyli had worked on her more than once to heal the external scars she'd sustained from battling as a gryphon while in the realm where she'd been captive. She appreciated not having to stare at a reminder of her imprisonment every day, but now she had to figure out how to repair the internal scarring.

If she told Garwyli her Belador powers were fading, he'd feel as if he'd failed her.

So would Storm after all he'd done.

She strolled forward, stepping over downed trees, which seemed odd since the Treoirs controlled everything in this realm.

Maybe a dead tree made the landscape seem more natural.

Unlike a dead gryphon.

How could she convince Daegan to allow her to return to Atlanta?

She couldn't walk around in real daylight due to her body's lethal reaction to sunlight, which meant she'd return to walking the streets of Atlanta at night. Just like before.

She ran a hand over her damp hair and turned to another problem she had to tackle.

Bonding.

Storm believed once they formed a powerful connection, he would be able to help her find her gryphon again.

Opening a bond meant energy flowing both ways. If his powerful energy traveled toward hers to unite, then what happened if her corrupted energy flowed to him?

When he explained bonding a while back, he'd said they would be eternally connected.

She'd asked, "What if I die? Would you die, too?"

He'd said yes without hesitation.

She would have too when she only thought about following *him* into the afterlife.

As she emerged from the tree line, she searched across the wide field between her and the castle. Storm stood patiently waiting for her.

Her stomach twisted at her next battle.

She could no longer avoid discussing the bond.

CHAPTER 5

A KNIFE OF GUILT DUG INTO Evalle's chest as she avoided meeting Storm's gaze from where he stood on the castle steps.

He tracked her like a heat-seeking missile from the moment she stepped into view. Surprisingly, he'd stood firm when she paused halfway across the field to watch the gryphons fly far above her head.

The giant beasts swooped in and out of puffy clouds floating across a powder-blue sky.

Garwyli had to be behind Storm staying put and not rushing out to check her wound.

That druid would forever be dear to her after aiding Evalle to return something precious to Storm—his soul. He reminded her of a grandfather, based on what others had described of theirs.

She'd never had one, but if she did she'd want him to be like Garwyli. What a kind soul to believe she really could call up her gryphon again.

At some point, she had to accept the reality she could no longer shift.

Watching the rhythmic flow of the colorful gryphons move gracefully back and forth mesmerized her.

Just one more time, she wished to shift again and take flight.

Her cruel conscience said, *Not happening so let it go.*

Not bad. She'd admitted the inevitable to herself and hadn't fallen into a fetal position.

A high-pitched screech ripped through the air.

Her heart pounded wildly. That sounded like Feenix.

He couldn't fly that high, could he?

She recognized the golden-headed gryphon as Bernie. He would never harm Feenix. But that second one, Ixxter, better known as the jerk of the pack, had bullied the others in the past. She'd thought that was behind Ixxter after she'd helped Tristan rescue him from being tortured. He wouldn't hurt her gargoyle, right?

Ixxter knew she'd ... her thoughts slammed into each other.

She'd do what?

Not a damn thing. She held back a scream of frustration. Then she remembered she could talk to them telepathically.

She shouted mind-to-mind. *Bernie. Is Feenix up there?*

The golden-headed gryphon had been gaining altitude when he swung around and looked down. *Evalle?*

Yes! Where is Feenix?

I told Ixxter not to take him up but ...

Liar, Ixxter charged in his Slavic accent. *You're the one who said he needed to stretch his wings.*

I'm not the one who took him higher, Bernie argued.

Don't be a pussy tattletale, Ixxter accused as his gryphon blindsided Bernie.

Evalle glanced at Storm who had started down the steps.

She had to deal with this.

Storm dealt with enough and this was her territory. Lifting an arm, she held a palm out, asking her mate to wait.

Storm did, but he didn't retreat. Just stood there watching with arms crossed.

Turning her head up, Evalle sent another telepathic message. *Where is Feenix, Ixxter?*

Having good time, he sent back in his thick Slavic accent.

Another screech higher up had the hair standing on Evalle's arms. She would use every last ounce of her energy to bleed that gryphon if anything harmed her gargoyle.

She sent back. *That is not his happy sound, asshole. If you...*

At that moment, a small green shape came spiraling down from way up, passing Bernie and Ixxter.

Bernie broke free, but he'd never catch Feenix.

Evalle called up her kinetics and pushed her hands up to slow her baby's descent.

Nothing happened.

Panicked, she screamed telepathically at them, *Get Feenix!*

I'm trying, Bernie called back. He'd flipped over and started flapping his wings in a wobbly dive.

Feenix's wings weren't even fanning the air to slow himself. He didn't look alert.

Ixxter folded his wings and barreled downward. His larger body dropped like a boulder.

Evalle yelled, "Feenix, fly! Open your wings."

No response.

Her stomach clenched.

Seconds slowed to microseconds.

Too close to the ground, Ixxter spread his black wings that caught wind with a yank, slinging him sideways toward Feenix. A giant claw extended and snatched Feenix out of the air right before Ixxter banked inches above the ground. Flapping hard, he shot up then circled to come back around and land fifty feet away. Covered in black and red feathers, his huge chest heaved hard breaths.

Evalle ran toward Ixxter's gryphon. "*Feenix!*"

The gryphon lowered Feenix, but Evalle got there to scoop up her gargoyle before he touched the ground.

She backed away, giving him a little shake. "Come on, baby, wake up." She could feel his little heart beating and his chest move with fast panting.

Sounding out of breath, Ixxter spoke in her head. *He is not dead. Just disoriented from flying high. Maybe could not breathe or something.*

She flashed the gryphon a look of death.

What happened to your kinetics, Evalle? You should have saved gargoyle.

That shoved guilt deeper in her chest. She hadn't been able to protect Feenix. Words stuck in her throat along with the need to lash out in frustration. She bit down to hold all that back.

Everyone would panic the minute she sounded upset and come rushing to help.

Feenix opened his bright orange eyes, pulling her attention back to him.

"Evalle?" He gave her a gap-toothed smile.

She could breathe again.

Feenix looked up and around. "Where ith Bernie?"

She hugged her gargoyle and Feenix forgot about Bernie. He used a chubby paw to pat her back. "You mith me?"

Swallowing, she said, "Always." She pulled him back to face her. "What happened?"

"I fly." His eyes glowed with excitement.

"Why did you sound scared?" She had to ask Feenix questions he could answer with his limited vocabulary.

He looked up again then back to her with a worried face. "Too high."

Ixxter broke in telepathically. *That is because he is not familiar with flying so much. You can not keep something with wings locked up.*

That dig cut to the bone, but she managed to hide her reaction. If she sounded defensive, Ixxter would take it as a win.

Bernie's silver-feathered gryphon landed and walked to the side between her and Ixxter. Having a golden eagle head marked him as special, thought to be one of the more powerful gryphons until he shifted into a scrawny little guy who feared his own shadow. His rambling voice came into Evalle's head.

I'm sorry, Evalle. Feenix kept flying a little higher every time I saw him take off. I thought he might enjoy some exercise, but I didn't mean for him to go that high.

Shut up, Bernie, Ixxter cut in. *You're just pissing Evalle off more.*

I'm not the one she's pissed at, Bernie countered telepathically.

Both gryphon gazes cut to her.

She kissed Feenix's head, careful not to let one of his horns stick her. Then she put him on the ground and turned her fury on Ixxter, who had taken Feenix too high.

Feenix had not feared gryphons from the first.

He thought they were big playmates.

Some might be, but Ixxter thought he knew better than anyone else.

She would normally be thanking someone for saving her gargoyle, but she wouldn't rush in with appreciation when Ixxter had been the one to put Feenix at risk.

She continued with telepathy since these two couldn't speak out loud in this form. *What the hell were you thinking, Ixxter?*

That your gargoyle deserved some freedom.

That's not your decision to make, she sent back with a load of anger.

So is better to keep him locked in box?

She gave up and shouted out loud at Ixxter. "He's never been put in a box. He has an entire floor of a building as a playroom."

Ixxter's growl was the only warning before energy pulsed and the black gryphon shifted into a man who towered over her. He wasn't particularly attractive, but he had a beefed-up body that belonged to a Spartan warrior.

His gaze skated past her. "You need your hand held?"

She looked over to see Storm walking her way again.

Dammit. She shook her head at her mate.

That didn't go over well, but Storm paused fifty feet away.

Adrianna had just climbed the castle steps and stood quietly, taking it all in.

Guards had paused then shifted their stance as if ready to come to her aid. She appreciated everyone more than they would know, but she could still make her own decisions.

Everyone tried to keep her calm. They didn't want to upset her.

She didn't want calm. Her body shook with unspent fury. She wanted to bust out her gryphon and teach Ixxter-the-bully a lesson.

But that wouldn't happen, would it?

Turning back to him, she checked on Feenix who had hooked an arm around her leg and nibbled on the tip of one claw.

"You owe me apology," Ixxter demanded.

"What?" Evalle curled her fingers to hide the trembling.

Too shy to shift in front of women unless he had clothes handy, Bernie could only speak telepathically. *You should apologize to Evalle and keep the peace, Ixxter.*

"Shut up, Bernie," Ixxter said out loud. He hit his chest with his fist when he said, "I save gargoyle and she yells at me."

She'd been giving him a chance to explain. "I owe you a fist sandwich, Ixxter." She crossed her arms. "You should take Bernie's advice. It would be a nice change to see you act like a normal, uh ... "

"Human being? Is that word you look for?" Ixxter sneered. "I am normal for gryphon. I did nothing wrong. Apologize." His shoulder muscles bulged when he hunched his back and stepped in to meet her.

Evalle shoved Feenix further behind her and hoped Storm

stayed back. She had no intention of fighting Ixxter, but she wanted him to know he couldn't intimidate her. She might have lost some power and strength, but she still possessed the ability to win a verbal argument.

Ixxter had to acknowledge that he'd taken a risk with Feenix and scared her baby.

She needed one win.

Who was she if she couldn't gain that?

In a blast of energy, Tristan appeared in human form between them and shoved a palm hard at Ixxter who rocked back two steps.

Evalle swiped hair off her face.

Just great. Saved again.

No Belador or Alterant-gryphon would look at her the same after today. They'd all been tiptoeing around her as it was and now Tristan had come in like a principal breaking up a schoolyard argument over a toy.

Wait, where was Feenix?

She twisted around looking for him. Her gargoyle tapped the bright blue petals of a flower growing close to the ground.

When she turned back, Tristan first took in Ixxter then arched an eyebrow full of question at her.

Speaking loud enough for Bernie, Ixxter, and Evalle to know they were all being addressed, Tristan asked, "What the hell started this?"

Evalle snapped, "Ixxter," at the same moment her opponent shouted, "Evalle."

Tristan held up a hand for silence and turned to Bernie but said nothing. That meant those two were conversing telepathically and Tristan had chosen to shield his words from Evalle and Ixxter.

Nodding as if to end their conversation, Tristan faced Ixxter and Evalle, saying, "Bernie tells me they were flying with Feenix."

Ixxter snarled, "Bernie squeals like little girl."

Bernie's gryphon made a threatening sound.

As the leader of the Alterant-gryphon pack, Tristan made a louder growl adding, "Everyone shut the fuck up for one minute so I can sort this out. I called to Petrina who has been teaching Feenix how to maneuver. My sister said she left when you showed up, Ixxter. She didn't want to get into a conflict." Then Tristan grumbled under his breath. "Must be nice to have that choice."

"Evalle owes me apology," Ixxter shouted.

"So you're the victim?" Evalle asked, lifting her hands in disbelief. She kept up her angry mask, but leave it to Ixxter to point out how she'd failed Feenix. Had Feenix been longing for a chance to fly in the open? Her sweet little gargoyle had seemed content, but it was her job to know what he needed.

Tristan shook his head. He probably regretted agreeing to take over leading the gryphons from Evalle.

She crossed her arms, losing patience, but she'd conceded the position of pack leader to him. He'd earned everyone's respect, including hers. He might not have the most diplomatic style, but he'd been sorting through gryphon issues for months when she'd been in Atlanta and she would not undermine his authority.

Ixxter gave Evalle a dark look but stopped mouthing off. Good to see that jerk could show respect for Tristan as well.

Sounding tired, which made sense because Tristan must have just teleported back from Atlanta and into this mess, he started again.

"As I was saying, Bernie indicated that Ixxter took Feenix to a higher level than Petrina had set before leaving." Without slowing, Tristan said, "Stop shouting in my head, Ixxter. She may not be your leader, but she's my sister and I trust her word. She warned everyone to be careful with Feenix. Sounds like *you* owe Evalle *and* Petrina an apology."

Ixxter cursed and said, "You are fools. Gargoyle is testing wings. He would go too high at some point. What would happen if one of us is not around when he tries? I tell you what. He falls like rock and hits ground. I did you favor show him not to go too high. Now he knows." At that, Ixxter exploded into his gryphon and flew away.

"*Ikther?*" Feenix asked in a forlorn voice. "Where go?"

Evalle squatted down in front of Feenix. "He went home for a bit." Ixxter's words kept banging around in her head. She had to ask, "Did you go too high, Feenix?"

He nodded with droopy eyes. "Yeth."

"Are you going to do that again?"

"Noooo. High not good. Ikther tell me."

Shit. She hated to admit Ixxter had a point. In his own screwed-up way, he'd shown Feenix his limits and had made an impression all the warnings in the world would not.

In addition to that, Ixxter had been right.

She owed him an apology.

Her anger lost steam. She had a sinking feeling she'd failed on yet another front. Sucking up her pride, she called telepathically to Ixxter, allowing Tristan and Bernie to hear her words.

Ixxter, it's Evalle. You were right. I talked to Feenix and he said you taught him to not go that high again. I'm sorry if I overreacted.

Tristan gave her a pensive expression, clearly waiting on Ixxter's reply, too.

Ixxter said, *Thank you. I would not harm baby gargoyle. You should know that.*

Evalle sighed and sent back, *You're right. I should. I'll try to not judge so quickly next time.*

Is no problem, Evalle. We are only human. Ixxter's laugh followed that.

Evalle smiled.

Tristan cocked his head. "Did you understand what he meant?"

"Yes, he was making a joke. Consider that progress with Ixxter." She chuckled, relieved she'd fixed one problem.

Bernie must have said something telepathically to Tristan who waved him off. The gryphon took a few steps, flapping his wings and lifted off.

Tristan stepped over to her. "If you want to kick Ixxter's butt, come back in gryphon form. I have no doubt you'd take him, and I'll bring the beer."

She'd never be able to do that, but Tristan still treated her as an equal, which felt good. Smiling she said, "You're on. You look beat."

"Yeah, I have to go give Daegan a report on what's going on in Atlanta, then I'm taking a couple hours down time," he admitted.

"Hours? You could probably use a couple days."

"Not yet."

See? Tristan and the Belador teams back home needed help.

Feenix lifted a blue flower and waddled over to gift her with it. "For Evalle."

She put it behind her ear. "Thank you, baby."

He clapped his pudgy paws and made a chortling sound.

That washed away the last of her tension. Watching him play with the gryphons brought a question to mind she needed an answer for before she talked to Storm.

She wanted Feenix with her if she could get a day back in Atlanta, but this wasn't about her. It was about doing a better job making her gargoyle happy.

"Feenix, do you want to go home?"

She got her answer when his face fell.

"No. I good."

Evalle dropped to her knees. "Oh, baby, I didn't mean you had misbehaved. You've been wonderful."

He gave her his special grin. "Thay?"

"Yes, you can stay. Everyone loves having you here. If I go back with Storm for a day or two, would you want to go with us or stay here and fly?"

Feenix looked up, then at Evalle, then back up and at Evalle again. "Thay?" he asked, sounding unsure if that was the right answer.

She hated to leave him, but she wouldn't deny him this joy. She had one more idea for fixing her power loss, which required going back to Atlanta.

Smiling to reassure him, she said, "It's okay with me if you stay. I'll be back before you know it."

"Yes. Thay!" He clapped and waddled around as if dancing. A large yellow and white butterfly came floating by three feet off the ground.

Feenix grinned and lifted into the air, flapping just enough to follow his new playmate.

She called out, "Will you stay with the butterfly?" That might keep him close to the ground if the bug didn't fly into the woods or go way up in the air.

His orange eyes blazed at her in a quick glance. "Yeth."

Little bat-like wings stayed busy as Feenix angled to the side and banked to the right in a sweeping movement as he watched the butterfly and chortled the whole time.

Now *that* was his happy sound.

She had never flown with him.

He'd been cooped up in her underground apartment until she'd met Storm and eventually moved into their building.

A powerful energy approached slowly from behind.

Storm stepped up beside her. "The butterfly won't go any higher or leave this area."

She should have known Storm had been behind Feenix's new toy.

Tristan had started to walk off, but turned back to say, "I'm headed to meet with Daegan. He asked for you two to join us. By the way, Storm, here's your phone."

Storm caught it from Tristan's toss.

Evalle asked, "What do you expect him to do with that in this realm, Tristan?"

Storm answered, "I asked him to take my phone to the human realm in case I had messages from the twins or someone else."

"Oh. Good thinking." Evalle had the best mate to keep up with people like the pair of teenage male witches living in their building.

Tristan said, "Someone's been blowing up that phone the whole time I was in Atlanta today."

Storm frowned as he scrolled the multiple messages from the same number. "No kidding."

"What's going on?" Evalle asked.

"My uncle is trying to reach me."

"Uncle?" Storm had family? Evalle thought he had no one after his father died.

Why did she pick up irritation coming from him?

"Yes. No big deal. Let's talk later." Storm's grim tone held an angry undercurrent. He closed the phone and changed the subject. "Before we meet with Daegan, are you ready to go home?"

Yes, she was, but she'd told Storm she'd bond once they got out of Treoir.

His face held so much hope, she didn't know what to say. As much as she wanted to be with him in Atlanta, she couldn't bond with him yet. Not until she figured out what was going on with her powers.

Evalle admitted, "Sure, I'd like to go, but I don't think Daegan will let me leave until I'm battle-ready."

"I heard Daegan will teleport us."

"Really?"

"Yes, but not for you to be patrolling the streets."

Her heart dropped at confirmation.

"Evalle?"

She knew when she failed with Hoyt she'd lost her chance to return to duty, but deep inside she'd held a tiny hope of joining the teams again. Pulling her shoulders back and her chin up, she did her best to sound confident. "I'm ready."

Storm gave her a loaded look, but she hadn't lied. She was as much as she'd ever be, based on today.

When they reached the platform for the entrance to the castle, Evalle said, "Go ahead. I want to talk to Adrianna before we leave if the dragon really is going to teleport us."

He paused with the indecision she'd seen on his face too often lately but nodded. "See you inside."

Once the door closed behind him so Evalle knew he couldn't hear her words, she walked over to Adrianna and quipped, "Quite a show today, huh?"

The witch gave her a smirk. "You're lucky Storm hasn't locked you in a room yet. He's a hair from losing control."

Evalle put both hands on her head and slid them down to her neck, trying to wipe away another slug of guilt. "I know. I'm the worst mate ever. I have no idea why he still wants to bond with me."

Adrianna said nothing.

"Okay, yes, I know he loves me," Evalle said, smiling at the stupid comment. She hoped he still would if she convinced Adrianna to do something back in Atlanta.

"Love doesn't begin to cover what that man feels for you, Evalle. He's determined to bring your gryphon back. That's why he's pushing even harder to bond with you now."

"That's a problem." Evalle had wanted to share this with Storm first, but she'd like to give him some good news for once.

Adrianna lost her relaxed expression. "Why?"

Lowering her voice, Evalle said, "My powers are failing. My kinetics didn't work to stop Feenix a few minutes ago and ... " She paused to lift her right arm and show it to the witch. "These lines showed up this morning."

Leaning close to study Evalle's arm, Adrianna asked, "What do you think that's all about?"

"Have no fucking clue, to be honest. It may be coincidence, but they showed up this morning and now my powers are getting weak. I agreed to bond with Storm as soon as we got back to the human world. He has some special place he wants to do the ceremony, but what if my powers drain his when we do this?"

"That could be a problem."

Tristan's voice came into Evalle's mind. *Hurry the fuck up, Evalle. What are you doing?*

Answering the same way, she said, *I'm coming. Give me sixty seconds.*

Tick tock.

Hurrying to finish, Evalle said, "I have to get inside, but I have an idea of what might bring my gryphon back."

"Oh?" Adrianna asked with a load of curiosity.

"You said you didn't want to use Witchlock here in Treoir, but what about when we go back to Atlanta? Are you willing to try it out on me there?"

The witch's mouth fell open then closed. "I want to say yes, because I'd gladly help with anything I could, but I have no idea what would happen if I use Witchlock on an Alterant-gryphon."

"Understood."

Arching an eyebrow, Adrianna sniped, "You may understand, but Storm will unleash his jaguar on me if I harm you."

"You're not going to kill me, Adrianna. I know you have more control than that."

The witch looked around and moved her lips in some silent conversation with herself. She turned back with her voice in that perfect calm tone she spoke in most of the time. "Yes, I'm fairly certain I won't kill you, but you may shift into something other than a gryphon. You started out as a ... "

"A hideous beast," Evalle supplied. "I'm willing to shift into *anything* if it means hanging onto my powers. I don't want to be a liability if I bond with Storm."

The doors to the castle opened and Tristan called out, "Hey. What's going on?"

Evalle gave Tristan the evil eye. He crossed his arms.

Ignoring him, Evalle asked Adrianna, "Will you try?"

"Give me a minute to think. We'd have to do it before you bond.

Mixing my power with his is way too big of a gamble."

"Got it." Evalle took off, hoping Adrianna would agree to teleport to Atlanta with them.

CHAPTER 6

I T WAS TIME TO BOND.
Storm couldn't take another day watching Evalle struggle.

She came rushing into the castle foyer behind a grumpy Tristan. She jogged to Storm as Tristan continued another forty feet toward where he stopped. Must be waiting on Daegan.

She caught her breath and said, "I owe you an apology. I didn't say anything about training with Hoyt because I wanted to surprise you. Myself, too, but I kind of blew it."

How could he complain about that?

Still, he didn't want her going off on her own with a sword or any other weapon. What if he hadn't been there to heal her?

When not sure what to say, he fell back on a safe reply. He hugged her and dropped a kiss on her head.

She asked in a quiet voice, "What makes you think Daegan is really going to teleport us?"

"Heard he talked to Garwyli and changed his mind as long as you're not putting yourself in danger."

She smiled, which might mean agreement from another person, but Storm's lie detector gift lit up.

What was going on in that beautiful head now?

"Where does your uncle live?" Evalle asked, clearly shifting the topic.

"He's in Arizona."

"Do you need to see him?" She sounded excited at that idea.

"Not really." Storm hated to squash her interest, but the surprise trip he'd planned to Arizona for their bonding had not involved his uncle. He wanted to do the ceremony on land his father had spoken of with reverence.

Curiosity buzzed in her questions. "You aren't concerned that he's calling?"

Why wouldn't she let this go? His fault. He should've told her about Bidziil before now. Had his uncle not chased a dream of riches where his father fought to maintain the tribe's culture, his father might still be alive.

Evalle's frown reminded Storm she'd asked why he wasn't jumping to get in touch with his uncle. He brushed it off with, "I doubt it's anything significant. Bidziil is my father's only sibling. He's in the casino business. I met him one time. He wanted me to join his clan on the reservation. I said no."

"You're not close?"

"Hell, no." Just having to return the call annoyed him. The only thing important to his uncle was making tons of money. "I'll eventually contact him when I have time, because I owe my father's only family respect. I don't have to drop what I'm doing to get back to him."

He'd figure out what was going on once he returned to Atlanta.

Right now, he had one task, to bring joy back to his mate's eyes.

When Tristan angled his head to call them over, Storm caught Evalle's hand to get moving.

He said, "I want to take you home more than anything. I miss you. Miss us. I'm not asking for more than you can give, but I'd like some *alone* time with you just to be. I figure you're ready to get out from under an army of people watching over you."

She cocked an eyebrow at that. "You've been part of that army."

He gave her the truth. "I'll always be there for you, but will do my best to give you room to work out whatever you need to."

A wave of relief rushed from Evalle, which bothered him. She should know he'd meet any reasonable request she made.

Meaning she did not want to put herself in jeopardy.

Just before they reached Daegan and Tristan, Evalle paused to whisper close to Storm's ear. "I may never be the person I was before."

That had been a huge admission. The first she'd made about her outlook of the future.

And it had been pure truth.

Seeing her eyes glisten with emotion hit him hard in the gut. He brushed a strand of hair off her face and behind her ear. He'd never tire of touching her.

Running a knuckle down her cheek, he said, "You will always

be my Evalle, no matter what powers you have. You will always be the woman who Feenix calls home. You only have to find peace within yourself."

She didn't say a word at first, just held his gaze with her bright green eyes. He kissed her lightly, just enough for a taste.

That drew a lusty sigh from her he loved hearing.

After a moment, she gave him a sexy smile. "I have high hopes about going home, too."

That earned her another kiss.

He had no idea what would happen with her physically once she left the Treoir power base and returned to Atlanta, but Storm was thankful Feenix would be here so she could focus on herself.

Thinking of Feenix reminded him how it seemed she'd shoved her kinetics up to slow Feenix's fall from the sky, but nothing had happened.

Was she unable to regenerate her Belador power and strength after battling as quickly as she had in the past?

As they reached a round area of marble where hallways met beneath a tall ceiling, Evalle said, "We're here, Tristan. Where's the boss?"

"He'll be here. Better that we're waiting on him than the other way around."

In spite of Tristan giving Evalle attitude, Storm picked up guilt still rolling off the gryphon leader when Tristan got around Evalle.

Tristan had linked with her as she died and used the second of his three regenerations to bring her back to life.

No simple feat to perform with any person, but Evalle had been given zero chance of surviving if she teleported out of Abandinu's realm. She'd been warned the Noirre majik shoved in her body would rip her apart from the inside out.

Daegan had no choice but to teleport her along with the entire team as the realm collapsed around them. He'd even pulled out a dragon he gave his own blood to save. That beast remained contained beneath the castle to keep everyone safe until he remembered how to shift into a human form.

Just as Evalle's gryphon had been damaged, maybe that dragon would never shift.

When Evalle could no longer shift, Tristan believed he'd failed her.

Storm would never fault her gryphon leader for the gift of bringing her back to life.

Daegan appeared next to Tristan in a rush of energy. The dragon king had the powerful body of a man born in the time when bloody battles were fought with huge swords and other brutal weapons from two thousand years ago. He'd spent the majority of that time cursed into the shape of a dragon throne in the Medb realm. Storm had joined a team of Evalle's people to free him.

In return, the Beladors now had a powerful leader. Though rough around the edges sometimes, that dragon-shifter had proven himself worthy of following.

Tristan asked Daegan, "Ready for a report?"

Daegan said, "I will be in a moment."

Evalle appeared immediately interested in Tristan's mention of reviewing a report.

Before the dragon told her she would not be involved, Storm jumped in first to make it easier for her. "Do you need us in the meeting, Daegan?"

Evalle frowned at Storm. "Of course, he does."

Daegan shut that down immediately. "On the contrary, I'd rather you not return to duty right away, Evalle."

Storm sighed. Some things couldn't be avoided.

"I see," Evalle said, showing no hurt on her face, but Storm's empathic senses hadn't missed it.

In the following silence, Evalle's gaze shot to Daegan.

Storm took that as Daegan speaking to her privately via telepathy. Tristan appeared to also be waiting to find out what those two discussed.

She lowered her eyes, looking embarrassed, but nodded.

Had the dragon's abrupt way of dealing with things hurt her?

Evalle put her hand on Storm's arm. "Don't be angry. Daegan was only telling me he knew the result of my training exercise with Hoyt."

The dragon lifted an eyebrow at her.

Storm's senses pinged that she'd only told a partial truth.

Evalle must've caught the subtle expression on Daegan's face and admitted, "Okay, not *training,* but a battle test."

"A battle test?" Storm snapped out before he could stop himself. He would not criticize his mate in front of her leader, but damn. A battle test meant no holds barred.

No wonder she got injured.

He muttered, "What the hell was Hoyt thinking?"

She turned to him with a frown.

Shit. Should have kept that to himself.

Evalle said, "He was thinking to respect my request. I wanted to see if I was ready to do more than lounge around Treoir like a lazy houseguest." She paused and her gaze swept across everyone.

Storm offered, "I wasn't criticizing you."

Evalle held up a hand to take the floor. "Please don't. I'm not entirely back physically, but I am capable of explaining myself to all of you." She glanced at Storm, before continuing in a softer tone. "You are all incredible and I appreciate what everyone did to rescue me and since then." Her gaze shot to Tristan who stared at the floor, but she wasn't finished. "I won't break if you piss me off. I can handle your reaction if I piss you off. Just don't tiptoe around me. It makes me feel like I'm living outside the group."

Tristan eyebrows shot up. "Can't blame me with that."

She laughed, surprising Storm with the sound, and said, "You're right, Tristan. You have never coddled me, and I thank you for that."

Her gryphon leader nodded.

Brina, the Belador warrior queen in her twenties, came waddling in with her new husband, Tzader. He held her arm as if she didn't possess the power to teleport if she stumbled. Wild red hair flowed behind her and a gown of green and gold covered her double baby bump.

She stated, "I'm here."

Daegan said, "I told you it wasn't necessary to join us, niece. This is not a meeting. We'll do that at the round table."

"Duly noted, uncle," Brina replied, undeterred.

A few years older with skin the color of dark mahogany covering a stocky body carved with solid muscle, Tzader shook his bald head at Daegan in a silent "let it go" message.

Daegan asked Evalle, "Do you have anything else you'd like to say, before we move on?"

"As a matter of fact, I do. Storm has something to do in Atlanta and I'd like to join him." She paused to say, "I will honor your order to not return to duty, Daegan."

When the dragon king dipped his chin in acknowledgment, Evalle added, "Feenix wants to stay and it warms my heart that he's so happy visiting. If it's okay with you, I'd like to give him a little more time. I'd appreciate everyone keeping an eye on my gargoyle."

Tristan said, "Done. He's welcome any time and he'll be safe." He seemed to catch himself and glanced at the dragon king. "Right, boss?"

Daegan smiled at Tristan. "I support your decision and will do my part to watch over the little beast."

Evalle grinned at Daegan's teasing tone that made it clear the dragon held affection for Feenix.

Seeing Daegan continue to give Tristan support even over small things continued to turn Tristan into a tremendous Belador asset. Who'd have thought that would ever happen considering how Tristan had been the enemy when Storm first met him on the opposite side of a battle?

Everyone seemed fine until Brina piped up. "No. I want you to stay here and heal, Evalle. You could be attacked in Atlanta."

"She will not be harmed," Storm stated, allowing no argument on that point.

Speaking in Daegan's direction, Tristan offered, "I could have a security patrol keep an eye out in the area of their building."

"I don't need anyone watching Evalle when I'm around," Storm said with enough force to make it clear to all.

Evalle snapped, "Tristan?"

"What?"

"No coddling. Remember?"

"Sorry. My bad."

All the conflicting comments drew a frown from Daegan.

No one knew better than Storm that Evalle would feel responsible for causing friction among her friends.

Right on cue, Evalle said, "I didn't mean to—"

Storm debated over jumping in to say more or leave Evalle to fight this on her own after she'd just put her foot down with every one of them.

Tzader interjected, "No one is going to argue that Storm is an unmatched protector, Evalle, but I'm with Brina. We want you here with us a little longer."

Garwyli came striding in quite fast for an ancient druid. His gray robe swirled around him when he stopped. "What's all this noise? How's a bein' to think with this racket goin' on?"

The old guy winked at Storm, stalling his next words until he saw what Garwyli had up his sleeve.

Daegan ordered, "Everyone calm down. You're distressing Brina."

"They are not, uncle. Don't be makin' me sound like a hormonal woman."

"But you are," the dragon king argued, clearly confused.

"I didn't mean to cause problems," Evalle finally finished saying.

Storm's heart bottomed out at her capitulation.

Garwyli inquired, "What problem might you be talkin' on?"

Turning a smile to her favorite druid, Evalle explained, "Storm needs to return to Atlanta, and I thought I'd go with him."

"How is that a problem?" Garwyli asked, directing his question specifically at Evalle.

She glanced at her friends and shrugged. "I don't want to upset anyone, especially Brina so close to having the twins."

"What you do will have no bearin' on her givin' birth," Garwyli said. He turned to Brina. "Am I right?"

Brina had opened her mouth as if to protest but huffed out a breath. "No. I won't be needin' her help. But I think—"

The old druid lifted a hand that demanded silence and not even the dragon spoke.

Garwyli brushed his fingers along the long white beard that hung to his waist. "We've all been takin' turns at givin' aid to Evalle. A body can weary of so much attention. She is a powerful woman on her own. I know ya want to be motherin' her, Brina, but you will have plenty to mother soon enough. I see no reason to keep Evalle here when she has a life to get on with back in Atlanta. Have none of you considered she may want a wee bit of time alone with her mate?"

Storm stifled a smile at the guilty looks Garwyli drew with that comment.

When no one spoke up, the druid asked, "Now, is there any other problem to be solvin'?"

"No, blast it." Brina walked to Evalle and hugged her the best she could with her round belly. She warned, "Just you be careful and come back soon or I'll be sendin' the dragon to find ya."

The anxiety that had pulsed from Evalle only moments ago dissipated. She smiled at Brina and told everyone, "Thank you for all you've done. Like I said, I'm leaving Feenix, so you know I won't be gone long. I don't want him to be any trouble."

"Of course." Brina sniffled and stepped back, trying to pretend tears weren't spilling from her eyes. Tzader hooked his arm around the shoulders of their Belador warrior queen and hugged her.

Daegan declared, "As Tristan said, your gargoyle is welcome and will be safe. If I hear otherwise, someone will lose their head."

Damn. Coming from Daegan, that was no empty threat.

Storm sent Garwyli a nod, letting him know he appreciated the help. The old guy laughed, clearly enjoying having his way. Storm's debt to that druid just continued to climb.

The dragon king announced, "If that's settled, are you two ready to teleport?"

Adrianna came hurrying in. "Wait."

Evalle turned with shock riding her gaze then relief.

What the hell was that about? Storm couldn't wait to get home and figure out a few things.

Adrianna slowed her rushed steps. "Me, too. Me, too. I've enjoyed the visit and I'll be back, but I'd like to be dropped at my house."

Looking around, Evalle said, "Wait. We need to get our clothes and things from our room."

Brina ordered, "Go on now. I'll have it all bundled and sent to ya."

"Is everyone finished filling my day with teleporting duties?" Daegan groused, but Storm caught a twinkle in the dragon king's eyes that said he didn't feel the least bit imposed upon.

"We're ready," Storm said then stood behind Evalle with his arms around her waist. Finally, they'd have some privacy.

The first thing they had to do was bond.

He suffered a moment of guilt over dangling the return of her gryphon by bonding, because he couldn't guarantee it. Still, that had to be better than giving up.

Adrianna yawned in Daegan's direction. "Thought we'd be there by now, dragon."

Daegan growled, "Irritatin' witch."

Treoir blinked out of sight.

CHAPTER 7

EVALLE'S EYES ADJUSTED QUICKLY TO the low light in the garage on the ground floor of their building. She'd spent so much time without her special sunglasses while in Treoir, she hadn't thought to ask Daegan for eye cover to wear in the human world. She had another pair upstairs though.

Storm stepped in front of her. "All good?"

She couldn't live the rest of her life with him worrying constantly that she'd not recover from her ordeal. If she gave him a big smile she didn't feel, he'd know it, but she could find a halfway point.

"*Yessss.* Did you forget my speech at Treoir?" she chided, adding a smile to soften the reminder.

"I heard, but this is the first you've changed realms."

"You've got a point." She looked at her body. "Two legs, two feet, two hands ... "

Storm caught her face with his hands. "One sexy mouth." He kissed her into silence. He'd always been able to do that.

Standing in their garage and smelling the familiar scents of home, she wanted to joke and return to their easy way of being together. Things had felt off between them these past ten days. Not *them*, but her.

Storm hadn't changed.

She'd been the happiest in her life with him, the only man she'd ever love.

She had to find that woman again.

He sighed and leaned down to meet her nose to nose. "Stop thinking so hard. Everything will happen in its own time. Let's get the elephant out of the room up front. No discussion of bonding tonight. Fair enough?"

Guilt-ridden over having avoided that conversation too long, she said, "I'm sorry, Storm, I—"

"Stop. Please, stop right there, sweetheart." He sounded frustrated, not angry. "You don't want me apologizing for not finding you sooner, then please don't you do it. You did nothing wrong. Nothing *is* wrong between us. I know you're hesitating to talk about bonding and maybe some other things. It pains me to watch you stress over us and to avoid me because of all that."

"No, I'm not." She wanted to bite her tongue as soon as the words were out.

He didn't say a word.

She closed her eyes and said, "Okay, big fat lie." Opening her eyes, she gave him the honesty she'd been holding back. "I love you so much there are no words and I have never doubted ours for each other, but when I was in Abandinu's realm with no possibility of ever seeing you again, I was actually glad we hadn't bonded. That sounds bad, but it's the truth. I can only imagine what would happen if you never found me again and had no way to unbond, if that's a thing."

His eyes fired up along with his voice. "Bond or no bond, I will always come for you and I will find you, no matter where you are. This world means nothing to me without you, but for right now I'd like to table the bonding conversation and enjoy being home. Agreed?"

She should've known he'd be fine about all of that, but leave it to Storm to state it bluntly and release a ton of pressure she'd been holding in. She could wait until tomorrow to meet up with Adrianna.

Since talking to the witch, Evalle made up her mind she'd tell Storm what she wanted the witch to do and ask him to support her decision.

That sounded pretty simple when in truth she kept imagining her mate stroking out.

Tomorrow. Adrianna hadn't been home in ten days either.

Tonight belonged to Storm.

Evalle moved her head to the side and leaned against his chest, wrapping her arms around him.

His heart pounded fast beneath her cheek but slowed the longer she stood in his embrace.

As his body formed to hers, he whispered, "You feel so good. I just want to hold you like this forever."

"Me, too." For the first time in days they were alone, truly alone. The twin boys Evalle and Storm had given a place to stay in one of the apartments on the second floor were still visiting Kit, a fierce human protector who treated those two male witches as her own.

Their other teen resident, Lanna, had remained in Treoir.

Just Evalle and the man she loved.

She relaxed against Storm's powerful body. All at once, she stopped fighting to regain who she'd been and to find her place in the Beladors again.

She stopped fighting period.

This moment belonged to the two of them and wouldn't have happened if she had not survived. She cursed herself for wasting even one second since then.

She had so much to live for, but had been too focused on losing her powers and gryphon to allow any other thoughts in.

Standing in her home with Storm brought things back into perspective. Time had no relevance in Treoir, unlike in the human world where every minute mattered for the people here. She might not be human, but she'd come face to face with her mortality when she'd thought she'd have a lifetime yet to live.

She might ... or might not.

The upcoming week would tell for sure, if not sooner.

In the meantime, she wouldn't waste one more minute she could spend with Storm.

He nuzzled her hair and murmured, "What's going on in that gorgeous head of yours?"

Evalle smiled. "You can't figure it out with all your gifts, Mr. Lie Detector?" She nipped his ear.

He slowed his hands for a moment then pulled her close again and sighed. "I will never get enough of feeling you next to me."

Just the sound of his voice wrapped her in comfort, reminding her there were no monsters to battle here. Not even the ones in her head could squeeze into this moment.

Storm had been right to bring her home.

He'd looked ready to argue with the entire Belador clan over taking her here until Garwyli shut down any dissent.

Home.

Even the air here tasted familiar.

She'd either find a way back to the person she'd been before her capture, or she'd figure out how to be a new version of herself.

If she didn't, she'd ruin what made her life with Storm special.

Snuggling her hips closer, she smiled over proof her mate was indeed happy to have her home.

He'd returned to being cautious around her in Treoir.

She didn't want that.

She wanted her man.

His heartbeat kicked up when she'd moved just now. He brushed hair away from her neck and kissed her. His words came out rough. "Be careful what you start, sweetheart."

She squeezed her eyes at the caution in his tone. They'd moved way past him having to take it slow around her in the early days. She'd been so messed up at first, it had pushed him back to tiptoeing around while she healed.

No more.

Her time in that vicious realm had been brutal, but she wouldn't allow it to steal one more thing precious to her.

Reaching deep for the playful side he'd always loved, she teased, "Is warning me to be careful the same as saying you have a headache?"

He stilled and didn't answer.

Damn. Had she sounded ridiculous?

That had been a stupid move, now Storm would feel uncomfortable around her. How could she screw up this moment when being intimate had always been so natural for them?

Gripping her hips, he lifted her in the air.

She grabbed his shoulders and stared down at him. "What?"

"You. What do you want?"

Heart pounding a crazy beat, she lifted an eyebrow. "Am I going to have to train you all over again?" she taunted.

He laughed and shook his head. "I've missed you."

She gushed out a breath of relief and admitted, "I've missed us, too."

He whispered words she couldn't translate.

Her pants unzipped and slid from her legs. She shuddered at the feel of the material pulled across her sensitive skin. Panic and thrill raced through her.

He ordered, "Keep your hands on my shoulders."

The tail of her T-shirt bunched and moved up slowly, brushing over her bare breasts.

She clenched her legs at the friction over her nipples. "Storm ... I need you ... now." That usually worked to get him inside her. The sooner that happened, the better.

"I need you, too, sweetheart. Do you trust me?"

She had a moment of worry. Storm's empathic sense would pick up any hesitation on her part, which meant he'd probably caught her worry.

Not an emotion that encouraged getting fully naked.

She held his fierce gaze, determined to show him she would meet him step for step in whatever he wanted to do. "Yes. I trust no one the way I do you."

She must've gotten it right and he picked up a different emotion this time. He gave her a seductive grin.

She matched it with her own sincere one. "Now, will you hurry the hell up?" she demanded, sounding more like herself.

"Hell, no. We're finally alone and I'm in no hurry."

"What if I am?" she argued.

"You'll like this better," he assured her. Then her panties slid slowly down her legs.

"You're killing me," she muttered, wanting to run her hands over her breasts and ease the ache or get her hands on him to return the torture. "You still have all your clothes on."

With another briskly spoken phrase, his jeans ripped and flew off him, leaving her commando mate in all his hard glory. He whispered and a condom slid over him. Her man thought of everything.

Heat pooled in her womb from anticipation alone.

He lowered her and she hooked her legs around him, anticipation building to slide into place. She couldn't be more ready, but he paused with her poised just above that moment of connection.

She would not beg. He had to give in, right?

But Storm showed no strain at holding her.

Her gaze locked with his for the longest seconds, then he lifted her just enough to bring her breast to his mouth. His tongue toyed with her nipples and she strained against him, trembling with the need to feel him deep inside.

He switched to the other breast, biting gently, but that sharp pinch had her shuddering hard.

Wrapping an arm under her, he used his free hand to reach between her legs.

His touch felt like the first time he'd made love to her.

She bowed back and clenched her legs hard, clamping her teeth tight to not plead. Her mate had gifted fingers that knew everything about her. He teased her until she lost all thought, clinging to the edge of sanity, waiting, shaking, then giving up and pleading.

His fingers changed pace, stroking and pushing into her. He shoved her beyond reason into a cloud of frantic sensation.

When she peaked, her muscles were as limp as overstretched springs.

Lowering her, he held her close, but she needed to be lower. The tip of his erection brushed over her sensitive skin.

"More," she mumbled, daring him to refuse her.

When he kept her just out of reach, she lifted her head from his shoulder and kissed him. She wanted the strength of her love to come through this kiss, to let him know they were still as solid as ever.

She might never be a powerful Belador again, but she could do this. Be Storm's mate.

He kissed her back as if his life depended upon this very moment. She got so engrossed she had a nice surprise when he lowered her until he pushed inside.

That dragged an honest moan from her.

He continued easing his way deeper in until he filled her.

That sensation described their relationship. Storm filled up all the empty places that had been dead inside her. His love gave her life.

He held her there and closed his eyes for a second. When he opened those beautiful brown orbs, he spoke in a shuddering breath. "This ... us ... you are everything I need."

She leaned in and kissed him with everything she felt for this man, savoring the way he returned the emotion with every touch. His tongue slid past her teeth to toy with hers.

When she took a breath, she said, "This ... us ... you are my reason for living. I love you."

He buried himself inside her and she hugged her legs tight

around him.

Moving in and out, he drove her back to the fevered pitch she'd been in only moments ago. She clawed at his shoulder, desperate for more.

She gasped, "Deeper."

On the next push, he buried himself and stopped, shaking with the effort to hold back.

Running her hands into his hair, she kissed him, tangling her tongue with his until they were breathless. When she could speak, she asked, "What are you waiting for?"

"You," he whispered next to her ear.

"I'm ready."

"Look at me, sweetheart."

She lifted her gaze. Her breath caught at the heat burning his. Without blinking, she gave him a sexy order. "Do it. Now."

He pulled out and shoved in again, this time harder and faster, never blinking. He held her gaze as his prisoner. Muscles in his neck stood out and his shoulders were solid as stone beneath her fingers.

She moved with him.

He pushed one forceful time.

Tension held her at the edge, then tightened, and snapped, freeing her from everything except feeling. Her body burst with pleasure. She rode the wave that broke hard then calmed.

In two more strokes, he gripped her with shaking arms and gained his release.

Nothing could ever match being in Storm's arms, feeling him connected to her emotionally and physically. She floated in the half-world of postclimax, indulging in the smell of them and their love.

Wrapping her arms around him, she smiled.

If Adrianna's attempt didn't work, Evalle's life might be different moving forward. If so, she'd have to figure out how to adjust and make the new her work.

Holding her with ease, Storm turned and walked inside, rubbing her back the entire time.

He'd be happy if she never stepped into the path of danger again, but he also knew how unrealistic that'd be for her.

She'd worry about that tomorrow once Adrianna had a shot at

using her power.

Evalle dreaded telling Storm, but she couldn't in good conscious go to the witch without him knowing.

When he reached the landing for their living area, Storm announced, "You know what I want now?"

Based on how hard he still felt inside her, she could make a guess. She squeezed him in reply.

"Clearly you and I are not on the same wavelength." He gave her a put-upon sigh.

Had she been wrong?

Lifting her head off his shoulder, she expected to see him confused or annoyed.

Humor flitted through his gaze.

Before she could come up with a snappy comment, he said, "Don't get me wrong, sweetheart. I'm always interested in another round with you, but I thought we'd grab some food. The food on Treoir is excellent, but I miss eating in the human realm."

Talk about the power of persuasion. "Now that you mention it, I'm starving."

He accused in faux hurt, "You'd toss me aside that easily for food?"

"Maybe." She grinned and qualified, "Depends on the restaurant."

"Six Feet Under?"

Her favorite restaurant. "That is a great big yes. I just got my fill of you ... literally," she laughed.

He moved his hips again, pulling out then sliding back in.

She groaned, "Screw food. I'll survive."

"Nope. You already passed on me," he teased. "Besides, you'll need your strength for what I have in mind later." Lifting her off, he held her until her legs were steady then suggested, "You go shower and I'll go back for our clothes Daegan is teleporting."

"I suppose, if that's the best excuse you have."

He leaned in to kiss her and dropped his head to a breast, giving a quick nip then licking it.

She yelped. "Thought you wanted me to shower."

"I do, but I want you thinking about me the whole time."

Never one to be outdone, she turned to leave, then called out, "Oh, I'll think about how you left me wanting. It may turn into a one-person party."

"Damn. You better not," he warned.

"Then hurry up," she ordered. It felt good to banter with him again. Normal.

Her kind of normal.

After grabbing clean clothes, she hurried through the shower, rushing to get ready and look extra nice for him.

If only she knew how to add pizzazz.

Lanna could make that happen.

Since the young woman wasn't here to help, Evalle would just do the best with what she had. She brushed out her damp hair with no choice but to pull it back in her usual ponytail.

When she checked the arm wound Storm had healed, her attention stopped.

The strange black lines that had started just below her armpit and moved down were now an inch longer. Searching her body, she located a spot on her thigh the size of her index finger, then another on her back. That one appeared six inches long and had a wider spread with the lines split four times.

Lifting her left arm, which hadn't been wounded today, she touched the black fractured lines there.

They extended another inch then divided into new streaks.

She snatched her hand back and stared hard for a minute to see if any of it moved again. No.

Had her touch made the line extend? Were the inky designs a good or bad sign?

She still didn't feel any sensation of her gryphon.

Pointing the same finger at a towel hanging on a rack, she tried to lift it off the hook using kinetics.

The towel lifted up and started toward her then dropped to the ground.

Crap. What had she thought? That teleporting home would suddenly return her body to its original state? Actually, yes. She'd expected her kinetic power to have recovered by now.

Was she losing that ability entirely?

Bile rushed up her throat.

Had coming home changed something about the lines? Maybe she was overthinking this.

The inky marks could be nothing more than a preternatural

form of varicose veins or a cosmetic issue.

Had Storm seen the new lines on her in the garage?

Or had showering caused more to appear?

She dressed in one of her vintage short-sleeved BDU—Battle Dress Uniform—shirts, jeans, and her boots that hid sharp blades for battling. She might not be facing demons any time soon but wearing them brought a level of normalcy for her.

Squirting a drop of lotion in her hand, she brushed it over her face. Her gaze returned to the black jagged streaks that reminded her of the root from a cartoon tree.

Her body had been declared free of Noirre majik, but ... what if they were wrong and she had residue?

A crazy mage had forced that majik into her damaged body and fed it into her bloodstream and organs while she'd been captive. What if these lines on her skin were signs of the dark majik trying to leach out ... or take over?

Would Adrianna's Witchlock fix this power drain or ... force whatever was happening to Evalle's body to escalate?

She had to sound convincing when she told Storm her idea, which might be hard when she had serious doubts herself.

CHAPTER 8

STORM FOLLOWED EVALLE DOWN THE steps from the top floor of Six Feet Under where they'd sat outside where the smell of fried fish had mingled with the fresh air. He'd enjoyed watching her eat her favorite meal at her favorite place. Getting in on a Saturday night had been tough, but worth the wait.

Eating late at night had been their norm in the past. It was good to slowly get their life back.

Ten minutes into the meal, he'd relaxed at his first respite from constant worry.

"I want to check on my Gixxer sometime," Evalle said over the crowd from a step below him. "I may be able to fix it."

"Sure, we'll do that and see what it needs. Can we do that tomorrow?" Storm cringed at the thought of showing her the motorcycle she loved for the first time since the intentional wreck that left her vulnerable to kidnapping. Evalle had the skills to repair anything on her bike, but Storm doubted anyone could return the mangled parts he'd shoved in a back corner of the garage to the bike's original look.

She stepped around people stalled on the stairs working their way up. "Tomorrow is fine."

At the bottom landing, patrons crowded the area between the stairs and the hostess stand next to the front door. Storm took Evalle's hand and wove their way outside.

Her fingers seemed warmer than normal.

He had to bite his tongue not to ask if she felt okay.

No hovering.

When they reached the sidewalk, Evalle stared at the cemetery across the street, then turned to him. "When are you going to call your uncle?"

"I plan to as soon as ... " Storm reached for his back pocket to retrieve the phone, surprised it had stopped vibrating.

No phone. Damn.

He'd left it on the table, under a napkin to dull the buzzing of another message. Why the hell couldn't his uncle leave him alone? If not for the damn constant sound, Storm wouldn't be standing here torn over leaving his mate even for a minute.

Evalle asked, "What's wrong?"

"Left my phone upstairs." He wanted to drag her back up so she would be close to him. That sounded stupid in his head.

Sending her up to the get phone would be a dick move even if the thought had been only to keep her safe.

"Want me to get your phone?" Evalle asked with a bit of confusion.

"No," Storm said, dismissing his mental battle and silently cursing Bidziil for creating problems. Again. "I'll be right back."

"I'll be right here," she countered with a wink.

Would she?

He had to get past this incessant fear of her vanishing again. Heading back inside, he passed a group of six diners on their way out. They congregated on the sidewalk, which gave him a little comfort for her to have people close even if they were humans.

He politely moved through the throngs as quickly as he could to retrieve the damn phone that probably had yet another message from his uncle.

The last one said he needed Storm's help, but the man still gave no hint as to what kind.

Before the kidnapping, Storm had intended to give his uncle a heads-up out of respect before he brought Evalle to visit his father's land for bonding. He had no intention of visiting the man.

Their ceremony felt too far away to wait for now after sensing less of Evalle's energy tonight when they made love. By tomorrow, she might be the one pushing to bond immediately.

His uncle could wait.

Had Bidziil forgotten Storm's status as a Skinwalker?

Storm had no desire to be unkind to his father's brother, but neither did he wish to encourage a relationship.

Rushing back down the stairs and getting cursed at for gently pushing his way through the crowd, he stepped outside. The six people he'd passed on his way in were still saying their goodbyes.

His blood pressure dropped significantly with the knowledge these people were perfectly fine, so Evalle had to be.

Circling them with the intention of asking Evalle if she'd like to walk for a bit, Storm stopped short.

No Evalle.

He clenched hard to hold back his jaguar from breaking free. The animal had been agitated the entire time Evalle healed.

Sucking in a deep breath, Storm caught her scent and his senses sharpened.

His nose turned him toward the massive historical cemetery. Taking off to follow her scent, he rushed across the street, not caring if anyone saw him turn into a blur of movement. He took the lack of screams or car tires squealing as a positive sign and leaped the stone wall to land inside Oakland Cemetery, which sprawled across forty-eight acres.

His natural night vision took over as he ran through long shadows thrown by moonlit monuments.

His jaguar raged to get out. Claws extended from Storm's fingertips. He forced the beast back down to let him lead in his human form.

Evalle's shout cut through the silence. "Drop that child and walk away."

An acidic male voice said, "You can do nothing to me, Belador."

"Guess we'll find out. I'll give you until the count of three to put the child down and vanish. After that, you're mine."

The bastard laughed. "You are no threat."

With Storm's keen hearing even this far away, he'd caught enough to be sure he wouldn't put her in danger by racing in. In twenty feet, he'd passed between two massive monuments and entered the area where Evalle evidently faced off with a preternatural who had a child.

Human? Probably.

Before Storm reached the monuments, Evalle snarled, "You bastard."

Storm lunged forward to find a Medb warlock on the far side of the area clutching a limp child against his chest.

Evalle slapped kinetic hits at two other warlocks emerging from a dark shadow on her left.

Her strikes weren't slowing them down.

Shifting would create more problems at the moment.

Storm allowed his claws to come out as he sped past Evalle, blindsiding one warlock and slashing his face apart. The high-pitched scream might bring a cop. Most civilians knew better than to rush into a dark cemetery after that sound.

Evalle spun and kicked, using the blades she'd released from the soles of her boots. But that meant her kinetics had truly failed her.

Not good.

Storm finished off the warlock he had by ripping his head free. Purple blood ran from the now headless corpse. He swung to face the mouthy warlock who'd started backing away.

Feeling his head jack out of shape with his jaguar pushing to shift, Storm snarled garbled words through oversized jaws. "Drop child or I eat you."

Storm took a step forward. Blood dripped from his claws.

The warlock must've realized he was about to be on his own. His eyes bulged. He dumped the little body and ran away.

Swinging back to Evalle, Storm wanted to let her finish off her warlock just to give her some confidence, but that damn Medb started chanting in an evil tone.

Black smoke circled him.

Fuck. This.

Storm pulled his jaguar back under control and called up his own dark majik. He slammed the warlock with a hit of Skinwalker smackdown.

The black smoke turned into a cloud of spikes that sucked tight around the warlock and smothered his scream until he finally died. He hit the ground as a shriveled black corpse.

Evalle had been in the motion of kicking the warlock when he turned into ashes. With nothing to hit for resistance, her motion sent her spinning into Storm.

He leaped away, but not fast enough.

Her blade slashed across his shoulder.

He hissed, caught his balance and spun to catch her from landing on her face. She gripped his arms, heaving hard breaths. Perspiration ran down her face and soaked her clothes.

She shouldn't be this winded.

"Dammit," she said, eyes on his bloody shoulder.

"No big deal."

She insisted, "I should've sensed the other two in the area and picked up their energy signature before they got that close. They trapped me."

He couldn't argue. That's exactly what happened.

One more sign she seemed to be losing ground with her powers.

The Medb coven had to be running wild in the city for three to be so bold. Or had their miserable goddess queen lost her ever lovin' mind and put out a hunt order for Evalle?

Storm had been in a Tribunal meeting with Daegan along with that Medb goddess when the dragon king made it clear he would make a statement out of any of his people being harmed again. He and Storm had been searching for Evalle at the time.

Not even the Medb queen could be that crazy.

Those warlocks had to be opportunistic, probably wanting to expose a gryphon to the public. With Evalle unable to shift, the joke ended up being on them.

Would there ever be an end to nonhumans wanting to capture and use Evalle for one reason or another? Not as long as they still thought she could shift into a gryphon.

He called up his healing, pushing power hard to rush the process. Anything to wipe the guilty look off Evalle's face. It must've worked.

She turned away searching for something. "What happened to the little boy the warlock had?"

Storm nodded across the forty-foot space. "By the tree. I wouldn't have let that Medb run off with him."

Rushing over, Evalle knelt down and picked up the little body, struggling to lift him as she stood.

Storm grimaced. With her preternatural strength, that boy should be easy to lift.

Hugging the child to her, she walked back to Storm. The kid had on ragged jeans, a T-shirt with cartoon images, and sneakers. Just some human child the Medb had snatched as bait.

Looking down, she said, "He looks to be about five. We have to find his parents."

No, the police had to do that.

He wanted his mate out of here and somewhere safe.

Storm suggested, "Can you ask Trey to send a Belador who's on the force? They can deal with the warlock bodies, too."

She said, "Good idea. I didn't think about that." She stood still, staring at nothing while she reached out telepathically to Trey.

Frowning, she glanced at Storm. "He isn't answering me."

Trey had ridiculous power when it came to telepathy and handled communications for the Beladors in this city.

He would not ignore Evalle.

Had he even heard her?

"Let me see if I can reach him." Storm pulled out his phone and gave Trey a quick rundown as soon as the Belador answered. Trey said he'd send in a cleanup crew and instructed Storm to meet a cruiser near the far end of the cemetery where they'd have less chance of being seen.

Taking the child from Evalle, Storm relayed the plan as he led them to meet the car.

"Did Trey say he heard my telepathic call?" Evalle asked.

"I didn't ask," Storm admitted, which was true. He hadn't wanted to start telling Evalle's people she had issues.

She could tell them if the time came for disclosure.

She walked along quietly, but her emotions churned up a cloud of anxiety. She admitted, "I might as well tell you what's been on my mind. I asked Adrianna to use Witchlock to see if she could jumpstart my power or maybe even ... my gryphon."

Storm had to bite down on his first reply of *hell, no.*

He maintained an easy gait, doing his best not to spew empty words about how everything would be okay once they bonded. He couldn't in good conscience say all of this would end well.

Her telepathy appeared to work in Treoir when she spoke to the gryphons outside and to Daegan inside the castle, but that might have just been a benefit of Treoir.

Could Adrianna's power do what he and Garwyli had been unable to accomplish?

Storm said, "I'm not crazy about anyone experimenting on you—"

She jumped in. "It was my idea, not hers. I asked her to do this."

"I understand, sweetheart. Give me a chance to finish."

Casting him an apologetic glance, she said, "Go ahead."

"I trust Adrianna to not do something to harm you, but she has yet to fully control Witchlock." He had to meet her halfway on this, though. After a couple more steps, he said, "I'll support you doing this if we bond first."

Evalle started shaking her head. "You have no idea what could happen."

"True. I still know you'll be stronger if we bond."

Her mouth set in a firm line as she walked a few more steps. She admitted, "I have a couple more lines on my body."

Shit. He had a feeling that couldn't be good news. "What do you think it means?"

"To be honest, I don't know, but it seems my powers are weakening so the lines might be a sign of losing my preternatural powers."

"No." He refused to believe such a thing.

"It could be, Storm," she whispered, her heart in her voice. "If so, we have no idea what will happen if we open a bond between the two of us."

Finally, he understood why she'd been pulling back from bonding. "I can't make you do anything," he said. "I would never *try* to either, but I'm asking you to not attempt this with Adrianna until we bond."

Evalle ran her fingers through her loose hair. "She won't do it if we're bonded. Adrianna is concerned about what her majik would do to yours."

Well, shit. He still believed Evalle would need his power to experiment with her body. He'd take his chances and argued, "I'm strong enough to deal with it."

She stopped, forcing him to turn to her. "You can't know that, Storm, and I can't lose you."

"I can't stand by and watch you take this risk when your powers aren't a hundred percent." They were getting nowhere with this. He feared few things, but Evalle running out on her own to solve this terrified him.

He needed her agreement on one thing now when they could discuss it with no pressure. "I meant what I said a moment ago about not forcing you to do anything, sweetheart. Ever. That being said, I want to ask you for something since every step forward with all of this is one into the unknown."

"Okay, what?" she asked in that worried voice that tugged at his heart.

"If you reach what you feel is the end of your power or face any moment you think you can't overcome physical issues, I want your agreement I can open the bond no matter where we are or what we're doing. Please don't make me stand by and watch you lose ground without trying to help, because you wouldn't want to be in that position."

They stood there for a long stretch until she said, "I agree to allow you to bond us if I'm in dire straits. You're right, I would want the same opportunity in your shoes."

His heart relaxed with at least that. His mate had a streak of honor a mile wide. He leaned across the kid he carried to give her a kiss. "Thank you."

"You're welcome, but I'm not happy about waiting to get with Adrianna."

Win one battle at a time had been his constant mantra around Evalle, but this situation was unlike any other. She was no longer the skittish female he'd first met. He respected his mate's inner strength, which was why he addressed a potential problem. "We can make getting with Adrianna happen, but I would appreciate it if you agree to not go to her unless we're bonded."

Indecision rode across her face while he held his breath. Frowning, Evalle released a loud sigh. "Okay. I'll wait to give her a shot until we're bonded."

He picked up a wave of disappointment. She tried to hide it with a polite smile, but guilt climbed his neck at letting his mate down. He'd give this woman the world on a string if he could, but couldn't bend on her going to Adrianna without the benefit of his energy and majik.

Preternatural powers were different for everyone.

Evalle needed to be strong enough to test hers.

As they reached the end of the cemetery, an Atlanta police cruiser sat parked with a uniformed officer standing nearby on the sidewalk. Preternatural power radiated from the thirty-something man with a narrow face and sympathetic eyes.

Belador.

Alterants like Evalle normally carried more power than her Belador teammates.

Now that Storm had exited Treoir, he had to admit he'd hardly felt Evalle's energy.

The officer took the little boy from Storm and said, "We have a missing child description from the projects not far from here that fits him. Was he hurt?"

Evalle said, "No."

"You have any idea why he's unconscious or when he'll wake up?"

"Not really." Evalle added, "Warlock might have used a sleep spell on him."

The little boy mumbled something like he was coming around.

Noticing the child starting to wake, the officer laid him in the back seat of his car and covered him with a blanket. Turning back, he asked, "You're Evalle Kincaid, right?"

"Yes." She turned toward Storm. "This is my mate, Storm."

Storm shook the man's hand then the Belador officer asked, "Do you know why that kid was grabbed? I'm keeping Trey up to date on any nonhuman intel."

Evalle explained, "A Medb warlock used him to lure me into a trap. Storm scared the one holding the boy. The warlock dropped the child and escaped. He killed the other two."

"*We* killed them," Storm stressed.

Evalle said nothing.

The Belador gave a nod. "Okay, he may be safe now if that family wasn't the target, but I'll have one of our people keep an eye on them until we feel sure no one is coming back around." He added, "Thanks. Be careful who you trust."

Storm asked, "What are you talking about?"

"Not sure you've heard, but rumor has it some of the bounty hunters working for VIPER as agents are teaming up with the Medb. We have no idea who's on our team these days unless they're Beladors or declared allies of the dragon."

VIPER represented a coalition of nonhumans who protected humans from predatory preternaturals. The organization seemed to be breaking apart at the seams. Everything Storm heard translated into more danger for Evalle.

She stayed inside all day to avoid the sun.

He couldn't expect her to hide at night from a threat. Shadowing her everywhere as a bodyguard wouldn't go over any better.

Hell. He'd made a mistake by bringing her back here.

When the cruiser pulled away from the curb and drove off,

Storm's phone rang. In his hurry to silence the call, he hit the wrong button, making it live.

A human wouldn't have heard the words as clearly as Storm when a voice said, "Storm, if that's you, don't hang up. This is Bidziil."

His uncle. Dammit.

Evalle gave him a just-do-it look.

Storm lifted the phone. "I can't talk right now, Bidziil. This is ... I'm busy at the moment."

Clearly ignoring Storm's words, his uncle rushed ahead. "Please listen, Storm. This is important. Critical even."

Evalle watched him silently.

Storm had his hands full trying to navigate what was going on with his mate and figuring out if he should take her back to Treoir. Was it too much to ask for her to be free to move around without expecting an attack or trap constantly?

Hell, was it too much to ask for his uncle to stay out of his hair? Storm's father would expect him to show respect no matter how much Bidziil annoyed him.

He told his uncle, "I wish I could help you, but—"

"Storm," Bidziil interrupted, his voice pleading.

Trying to sort this out so he could move on, Storm asked, "You have how many hundred employees? Why do you need me?"

Evalle's eyebrows lifted in curiosity.

He'd never talked about his uncle, because their world didn't involve him. His father had been disappointed in how Bidziil and the others failed to preserve the Dine culture.

Storm had kept his presence in this country secret from his uncle until he'd had to contact Bidziil for help. That had been back when the Tribunal sent Evalle to the middle of a South American jungle where she'd faced off with a monster.

For her, Storm put his anger and ego aside to gain resources he needed immediately.

Storm could locate her, but to actually reach her quickly before the monster killed her, he'd needed access to a private plane.

Ironically, the monster had been Tristan, the same one who just revived her days ago when no one else could.

With all that in mind, Storm did owe his uncle something, but it shouldn't require going to see the man.

Feeling the weight of his father's expectation that his son would step up to help family, no matter what, Storm reluctantly asked, "What's going on, Bidziil? Maybe I can send some people."

"I wish this was that simple, but it's not. We can't have outsiders here. If you'll just come out, I can show you why I need you specifically. I can't talk about it over the phone. I don't trust electronics with what is going on."

What about the electronic slot machines filling his uncle's casino?

Guilt banged around inside Storm.

Bidziil hadn't hesitated to provide funds for the private jet he claimed had been paid for with money that belonged to Storm anyhow. His uncle had evidently been managing it for Storm's father.

Swallowing hard, Storm wrestled with trying to do right by his uncle, but he couldn't get past a long-held grudge. Storm's father might not have gone to South America and died there if not for Bidziil pushing so hard to take their clan in a direction his father opposed.

Had your father not left the reservation and moved to South America, you wouldn't have been born or met Evalle, his conscience reminded him.

Or had that voice been Storm's spirit guide, Kai?

"Storm, you there?" Bidziil asked quietly.

"Yes."

His uncle spoke hesitantly. "I didn't want to call you, but ... your people need you."

They weren't *his* people. Not really.

He had Dine, or Navajo, blood and knew some of the culture, thanks to his father, but he'd been raised in the Ashaninka tribe.

Storm asked, "What if I come out in two weeks?"

"Two hours is too long," Bidziil replied in a grave voice.

"What? I can't drop everything I'm doing and fly out for some problem you aren't willing to explain," Storm argued, frustration boiling in his words.

Heaving a long sigh, his uncle said, "I understand. When we lose another one, I can at least say I asked. Goodbye." The call ended.

Evalle said, "If you squeeze that phone any tighter it's going to be plastic confetti."

Storm opened his palm to see the sides of the phone crushed. Wiping a hand over his mouth, he stared at the ground and thought back over the call.

When we lose another one ...

That sounded dire. Had his uncle been talking about someone dying?

That man had a team of people who leaped when he spoke. He had enough money to hire an army of doctors if his medicine man couldn't cure someone. Why would his uncle not allow strangers in when he'd opened the tribe's life to the outside world?

Your people need you.

Storm's father would've dropped what he was doing to return to this country, regardless of any difference with his brother, if he thought he could save even one tribal member.

His father would expect no less from Storm.

It was hard to swallow, but Bidziil had done the same for Storm.

Still, why couldn't his uncle explain more over the phone? Storm could get people in place to help, but right now he had one primary concern.

The impossible task of keeping Evalle safe while trying not to smother her.

"Storm?"

He lifted his head at her soft voice. "Sorry. Got sidetracked."

"When Tristan delivered your phone in Treoir, he said someone had been blowing it up. Were all those messages from your uncle?"

"Yes. He's got some problem he'll only discuss in person."

"You should go."

Storm opened his mouth to argue that it was more important to be with her. He paused when an idea hit him.

Within seconds, he had a new plan and told Evalle, "You're right."

Relief floated through her gaze.

Storm didn't believe that emotion had to do with concern over his uncle, which meant it might be about Storm leaving.

They'd just enjoyed a pretty damn good return home. Why would Evalle be glad to see him go so soon? His mate had something else going on.

Something she wanted to deal with herself.

She'd agreed not to go to Adrianna unless she bonded with him first, but she knew a shitload of other nonhumans.

He was not going to negotiate one more agreement at the moment.

Neither would he push her to tell him who else she might be considering, but his mate wasn't fighting her battles, internal or otherwise, alone as long as he lived.

She knew this but fighting alone had been ingrained in Evalle from the beginning. Her mother died in childbirth and her father abandoned her the minute he saw bright green eyes and was told she could never be exposed to sunlight. He'd paid his sister to raise her, which had been nothing more than locking Evalle in a basement and keeping her fed for the money the woman received.

He understood his mate's need to heal her body and not put him at risk, but that didn't mean he wouldn't do his best to keep her safe while she tackled those issues.

Checking his watch, he said, "I'll call my uncle back and let him know we're flying out right away."

"We?" Her eyes flared with surprise.

He tested the water with a simple question. "Do you not want to go with me?"

"No, I mean yes, I want to go with you. I just thought ... it didn't involve me."

"Anything I do involves you." He gave her a quick kiss and said, "Let's go pack. I want to arrive in Arizona before daylight."

Everything Storm said made sense to him, but he couldn't shake the feeling he might be moving too quickly, as if something compelled him to fly out now.

He brushed that off as another bout of guilt, because his father would be disappointed in him if he didn't. He also rationalized that this trip would put Evalle halfway across the country from Atlanta, demons, Medb warlocks, bounty hunters, and any other nonhuman threat.

"I'm excited," Evalle said with forced enthusiasm.

Her smile triggered his lie detector ability, but he attributed all of that to how little she'd traveled and possibly a bit of anxiety over meeting his uncle.

She'd settle down once they were on the way.

Getting her out of here topped his priority list.

He had a solid plan that would keep Evalle far from preternatural harm and wipe away some guilt at the same time.

What could happen to her at a casino on a reservation in the middle of the desert?

CHAPTER 9

"WHAT IF SOMEONE WANTS AN ID when we land?" Evalle asked, running out of reasons to not join Storm on this trip. She had sixty feet left to come up with a viable idea before they boarded a Lear jet. The drive west of downtown Atlanta to Fulton County Airport, better known as Charlie Brown Field, had them on time to depart just after midnight.

Finally. When they landed, would it still be Saturday? Did Arizona use Daylight Savings Time? She was too tired to figure that out.

They'd arrive before daylight. That's all she needed to know.

Even if she'd dragged her feet packing, Storm would have made the jet wait. Inconveniencing others would have been inconsiderate, and she did want to be with Storm, but he could function far easier without her.

Hadn't the warlock in Oakland Cemetery proven that?

As always, Storm had an answer for everything. "You won't need ID for anything. Stop worrying. This will be fun."

She argued, "Your idea of fun has flaws. Remember when you tried to tell me camping would be fun?"

"Bad analogy. You haven't camped yet. You will enjoy it when we go."

She silently disagreed. Going to a reservation in Arizona didn't sound as if they'd be in a city and there'd be nonstop sunshine. Give her an urban landscape any time with some Georgia rainy weather on occasion.

At the moment, though, camping sounded much more appealing than flying in an airplane to an unfamiliar city and staying in a casino.

What would those people think of her wearing sunglasses all the time? How did women dress to visit a casino? Evalle doubted they wore clothes like her standard jeans, boots, and BDU shirts. What would his uncle think?

How could she be of help when she couldn't go outside during the day?

She could keep coming up with reasons not to go.

A new idea hit her. How many people could the jet hold? Fifty?

Regardless of the number, she could tell Storm they shouldn't risk her becoming claustrophobic. She might panic, then her gryphon would show up at the worst time and kill everyone.

Her heart fell. That had a major flaw.

Mr. Lie Detector would roll his eyes at the fabrication.

She hadn't felt any glimmer of her gryphon in Treoir and experienced little power at all in Atlanta.

The world was safe from a spontaneous gryphon shape-shifting event.

She'd agreed not to tap Adrianna's Witchlock, a power at the high end of the nonhuman food chain, without bonding first, but she'd said nothing about finding another way to fix her body before she lost all her power.

Neither would she bond without fixing her problems first.

Going to Arizona killed any chance of looking for a different option from someone she knew within the nonhuman community in Atlanta.

If she tried to back out of going for any reason, Storm would immediately cancel his trip and stay so he could be nearby in support.

She sucked at being a mate these days.

When they reached the jet stairway, Storm sent Evalle ahead to where a woman decked out in dark blue pants, a matching jacket, and white blouse welcomed her inside.

Murmuring her thanks, Evalle stepped past the woman and into the cabin where she paused.

The interior reminded her of what she'd seen in movies of a corporate-style jet with luxury furnishings. Beautiful cream-colored leather sofas with matching chairs were scattered along the length of the cabin, accompanied by polished wood tables and sidebars.

No people.

She amended her assessment to a *private* corporate jet.

Storm's hand cupped her waist. "What's wrong?"

"Are we the *only* ones on this flight?"

"Yes," he confirmed. "Why don't you pick where you want to sit?"

Drawing in a breath, she continued halfway down the aisle and chose a sofa. She sat in the middle of the soft cushions and accepted she had no way out of this trip.

Storm asked to have the cabin lights dimmed as the jet motored to the runway. When he settled next to her, he asked, "Okay, what's wrong?"

She considered her options, such as admitting she didn't want to make this trip. She'd earn the biggest jerk award. Storm had never hesitated to do anything for her or go anywhere for her. The truth was she had a case of the jitters.

He could fit into any setting with a change of clothes.

She could dress up in runway model garb and still stick out like a weed at a national flower show.

Storm ran a finger along her neck. "Okay, spill it."

As they made the turn to get into position to take off and accelerated, Evalle searched for any topic to avoid whining about taking an unexpected trip. "Are you rich?"

His eyes widened in surprised then he gave her one of his smiles that could turn her into putty.

She had no intention of getting naked with a flight attendant only a few steps away.

Storm quipped, "Took you long enough to ask me that."

Lifting her shoulders, she said, "I've never thought about how much money you had until ... now."

"Really?"

"Well, that's not entirely true. I mean, we live in a building in downtown Atlanta and you have other real estate. Plus, I did wonder how you found me so fast in South America and down on the southeastern coast of Georgia when you showed up in a helicopter. I couldn't believe you'd chartered one to meet me before I went to Cumberland Island."

His handsome face fell at that reminder.

Her empathic gift picked up emotions she'd label as stress from a bad memory. She'd given Storm the slip in Atlanta to protect him from a beast game she'd intended to enter alone. She hadn't wanted to go, but her former miserable goddess leader had forced her into that position.

Telling Storm would have put him in danger due to being a Skinwalker who'd be expected to battle.

Also, Evalle didn't want him with her when she had low expectations of walking away with her life or freedom.

As it turned out, she'd been right on one account.

Storm showed up when she'd have thought no one could catch up to her from Atlanta after her huge head start, but he had and accompanied her into the secret nonhuman battleground.

Then the Medb teleported her and other Alterants on site to the TÅµr Medb realm.

Power built and rushed around her.

Yep, bad idea reminding him of that time.

Evalle patted Storm's arm. "Power down. I don't want you to blow us out of the air." She added a smile, because he had unmatched control most of the time.

How often had her ability to land in a dangerous situation tested that control?

Too often.

He relaxed and she returned to her initial line of conversation, saying, "You were telling me about where you got the money to charter a private jet at a snap."

"I have my own that I've earned, but I also inherited some meant for my father, according to my uncle. When things got crazy down in South America before my father died and I came up here, he told me if I ever needed anything to go to my uncle. I had no plans to ever contact his brother."

"Why?" She'd like to understand the friction she sensed between Storm and his uncle.

Storm curled his fingers around her shoulder while he took his time answering. "My father and his brother fought over different visions for their clan, which is why my father left. He felt his people were losing their culture and the only solution people such as his brother brought in had to do with exploiting gambling on the reservation. My father died and I ended up a demonic jaguar created by the woman who used him."

"The witch doctor who shall not be named," Evalle quoted Storm in an understanding voice.

"Right. I can't help thinking he and I wouldn't have gone through all that if not for his brother's determination to turn clan land into high commerce. I wasn't happy to contact Bidziil when I needed funds, but he wired the money the minute I asked."

Now Evalle understood the guilt coming from Storm. She kept silent as he finished explaining.

"When I returned from South America, I went to see him in person to repay him. He told me the money was my father's and, therefore, mine. He'd been managing it all these years. I realized I owed it to him to repay that favor."

She thought about when a Tribunal had teleported her to a jungle in South America. "You needed money to find me, right?" She shook her head and looked away. "I'm not just a constant danger to be around, but an expensive mate to keep up as well."

His jovial mood flew out the window.

Storm came off the sofa and swung around, kneeling in front of her. He used a finger to turn her face back to him.

When she met his gaze, he said, "Do you think I care one bit about any of that money? I would burn it all in a bonfire this minute if I thought it would fix ... " His lips closed in a firm line.

"My gryphon?" she finished for him.

———————

Storm had to give her the truth. "Yes, I'd give anything for you to shift into your gryphon. You want honesty, so I'm not going to dance around that topic. I didn't ask to be a Skinwalker or to have the ability to shift into a jaguar with my demon blood, but ... losing a limb would be easier than my animal. My jaguar is part of me. I get what you're going through and will do anything in my power to help your gryphon return."

She smiled, but her eyes wouldn't commit. "I know that even without you saying it and love you for not pushing me or expecting me to just get over it. To be honest, I hesitated to come on this trip, because I want to be able to move on at some point and, if I stayed home, I could figure out my limits. It does weigh on me that I'm not at the point to fully accept what I can't do. For now, I'm going to try not to dwell over losing my gryphon and do my best to enjoy this trip."

Reaching for the right words were never easy in difficult times, but for her he would try. "I will always support whatever you decide, but I'm going on record to say I think you shouldn't put a time limit on determining if what you feel right now is going to be your status quo."

She listened with a thoughtful expression.

After a few minutes, he sensed her emotions evening out as if maybe he'd given her what she needed to hear.

He hoped so.

Silence sometimes offered as much comfort as words. Storm waited until she corralled her thoughts.

Lines formed at the bridge of her nose while she pondered. She drew in a deep breath and let it out slowly. "Remember the shaman you brought in to bless our house? Is he like Garwyli and you?"

Was she looking for someone else to heal her? Didn't she realize he would have found that person?

Storm gave her an answer he hoped met the point of her question. "Yes, that shaman could heal, but his gifts are more suited to calling upon protective spirits, like he did for our rooftop room. Garwyli and I possess stronger healing gifts than him."

She frowned. "Was he a medicine man from your father's tribe?"

Only Evalle would get that he didn't feel connected to his uncle's tribe in a way that would make them Storm's. "Shamans are often considered medicine men and he is of the same tribe, but not from my father's clan. They have a specific medicine man in the clan, unless he's died and not been replaced. Why?"

Huffing out a big breath of air, she said, "This will sound dumb, but I was wondering if he'd see a non-tribal member."

Storm considered that.

Did Evalle just want to have someone give her a spiritual reading? What harm could there be in her meeting with a Native healer? None that he could see. "Nothing you say ever sounds dumb, sweetheart. To be honest, I don't know if a new person is in place or if that person will agree to meet you, but I'll find out. My father said he grew up with a man who should've taken his place once he left."

"Your father was a medicine man?"

Storm hadn't realized how little he'd spoken of his father, but Evalle had no true blood relation she'd acknowledge so those conversations hadn't happened.

He explained, "Had he remained with the tribe, he would've been."

"That makes sense, considering the power from your Navajo side. What was your father's name?"

"Sani." Storm hadn't said it in a long time. "I got the impression he became the go-to person around his clan from an early age. You've heard people call someone an old soul."

"Yes."

"That's how I think he was considered in his youth. I inherited some of my gifts from him. He spoke little of his time before South America, preferring to tell me about my heritage more than his life growing up there. His power lay in his passion for Native culture he felt was being lost. That's what drove him to travel thousands of miles to settle with a reclusive tribe like the Ashaninka and offer his aid."

Storm still couldn't believe that witch doctor—his birth mother—had deceived someone as powerful as his father, but she used her majik well to hide her dark side.

That manipulative bitch also managed to trick Storm into being captured in an underworld demon realm. He could appreciate how his father must have felt when he realized he'd been used.

"I wish your father was here, Storm."

He returned his attention to the woman he loved, far more deserving of his emotions than the one who'd birthed him to be her personal demon. "I do, too. He would have loved to meet the woman who holds my heart in her hand."

For that, he finally got a real smile that kicked his heartbeat into high gear. But he wanted to return to where this discussion had been heading.

Maybe visiting Arizona and engaging with some of the locals would reignite Evalle's interest in bonding. They wouldn't be that far from the location where he'd wanted to perform the ceremony. He asked, "So you want to meet a medicine man, huh?"

"I guess. I mean he heals people on the inside, right?"

His heart did a nosedive to his feet.

A medicine man in Bidziil's tribe had very likely never encountered someone with a missing gryphon. Storm had to keep their presence as nonhumans a secret for the benefit of his uncle's clan.

But he also had to be careful to explain this in a way that didn't result in Evalle saying never mind and shutting down on him. "Yes, the tribe's medicine man's form of healing is to bring a person's body back in balance. That often includes healing songs."

Concern lit in her eyes. "Will he know I'm not human?"

"He shouldn't, because he is and my uncle wouldn't have shared that I'm a Skinwalker with any of the tribe."

"Your uncle knows that about you?"

"Yes. When I tried to repay him, he pushed for me to move there and join the tribe. I gave him a demonstration of how my eyes change and shared that I was an Ashaninka Skinwalker they wouldn't want around. That's all it took to drop the topic."

"Does he think a Skinwalker is a demon like you said the South American people do?"

"Demon or a witch." Storm shrugged. "Either is considered to be from the dark side. The Dine people honor the earth and all the bounty it offers."

"The *Dine*?"

"Yes, many of the tribe prefer to be called that instead of Navajo." He paused, thinking about what they'd encounter at the reservation. If the medicine man his father spoke of still performed healing for the tribe, he'd be much older by now and possibly less receptive to meeting with a woman who didn't belong to the clan.

The last thing Storm would tolerate was anyone denying Evalle a simple request, but at the same time he had to respect his father's people.

It dawned on him that he might have a way to make that easier to set up and also be better for Evalle.

Storm started, "Here's how I think it works most of the time." He clarified, "I'm not positive, because I'm not a member of my uncle's tribe and only know what my father taught me."

"Okay. I'm listening." Evalle sounded eager to hear more.

"You should actually meet with the seer first, because he or she is the one who determines in what way your Hózhó is out of balance."

"My what?"

He chuckled and moved back to the sofa where he could feel her close to him. "Think of Hózhó as your body and mind being in harmony. Once the seer has determined where the problem is, the person in question goes to the medicine man with what the seer has pinpointed. Then the medicine man uses that information to perform the healing."

"Huh. So the seer is like a specialist giving a diagnosis?"

Her genuine interest encouraged him to tell her more. "In theory, yes, but if I can arrange for you to meet the seer, it won't be like meeting a human doctor."

"Good. I don't like doctors."

Storm curled his fingers into a fist then relaxed his digits before he set his power churning again. A man working under the pretense of being one visited Evalle as a teen while she lived locked in a basement and that bastard had abused her.

The aunt and pseudo-doctor were both dead or Storm's jaguar would be roaring for a hunt.

Evalle almost shifted the first time in that basement, which scared the predator into a panic. He died upon impact in a single-car wreck.

Too nice of a death.

"A seer sounds more like you and Garwyli," Evalle speculated, dragging him back to the present.

Storm said, "Sort of, with the exception of the healing, which is left to the medicine man. Those two don't normally work together specifically as in the same location, but they do share the responsibility of keeping their clan healthy."

She tapped her chin. "That makes sense."

Now that Storm thought about it, he warmed to the idea of Evalle talking to a seer. Being a spiritual person, the seer might be open to a non-tribal member looking for help. His father had spoken of how the people he grew up around were compassionate and had an honest approach to healing.

Just talking to a seer could be beneficial for her psyche.

At this point, she had only two paths for moving forward. She either found a way to call up her gryphon or accepted that she'd never be able to again.

The latter possibility sickened him.

Storm made up his mind that Evalle would have her wish. She asked for so little.

He suggested, "If you like the idea of meeting the seer first, I'll find out about getting you an invitation. After that, if you still want to meet their medicine man, it will probably be easier than just asking out of the blue. Either way, I'll gain an audience for you."

"No, don't ask the medicine man yet," she hurried to say. "Meeting the seer sounds interesting." Then she sat up. "But first, I'll help you with whatever your uncle has going on."

"We can do both. Bidziil will be waiting at the airport when we arrive. Once I determine what's going on, I'll have a better idea of our schedule. As soon as his problem is resolved, we could stay a couple days, maybe take a break from the Atlanta preternatural rat race."

This would be the perfect chance to complete their bond. He hoped she considered it before the end of the trip.

"Sure, we could do that as long as Quinn or someone doesn't need us back home," Evalle said.

That hadn't been an ecstatic reply, but *one step at a time.*

He drifted a finger over her hair. "Good. I'd like to see more of this part of the country myself."

"We won't see much at night," she joked.

He leaned over and kissed her cheek. "I'll get a vehicle and put a protective spell over it to block the sun's rays like I did for my truck."

"Okay, great. I can't wait to see a new place with you." This time, her voice had a lift of excitement.

His chest muscles eased at hearing her sound more like the Evalle he knew.

Maybe having her involved in whatever he had to do for his uncle would fuel her confidence, which had taken a hit at the loss of her gryphon. Using her sharp wit and ability to sort through a problem could show her how her value went deeper than telepathy and kinetics.

Just in case those powers continued to weaken.

If he had to leave her alone during the day for some reason, security around the casino would be tight. More than that, no one in the preternatural world would know her location while they were with his uncle's clan.

He ran it all through his mind again.

Sounded simple and safe.

Why had a sliver of doubt burrowed into his conscience? He experienced that odd sensation again of questioning if he should be making this trip at all.

Evalle yawned and leaned over.

Storm closed his hands around her shoulders and moved her to his lap so she could stretch out. Her nocturnal schedule had been off since waking up in Treoir.

Once she drifted to sleep, Storm waved off the flight attendant heading his way, then dropped his head back and closed his eyes. With no idea what lay ahead of them, he could use a quick nap, too, evident by how quickly he fell asleep.

"*Storm?*" a soft female voice called from a distance.

Was that Kai?

Storm hadn't tried to reach out to his spirit guide in a few weeks. They normally met when he had a private moment, which hadn't been recently. When they did, he'd find himself in a pretty meadow with the sun shining, all composed by Kai.

She'd watched over Storm his entire adult life.

"Kai, where are you?" His words sounded muted. Could she hear him?

"*Storm, you must ...* "

"What, Kai?" Why couldn't he open his eyes and see her? Why was it so hard to hear her?

Kai's voice wobbled, "*... her ... spirit ...* "

"What?" Raising his voice never went well with Kai. She tended to call up a thunderstorm. "Kai? I can't see or hear you."

"You ... find ... Evalle ... dying ... "

Storm came awake, panting.

Evalle moved where she slept under his arm. She grumbled something unintelligible. He tucked a blanket over her the flight attendant must have spread across his mate.

He still couldn't catch his breath. His heart battered his chest.

Why couldn't he hear all of Kai's words? He didn't know, but he had definitely heard two.

Evalle dying.

What had he and Garwyli missed?

CHAPTER 10

WARM AIR MUCH DRIER THAN her humid Georgia in June met Evalle as she stepped off the jet stairway at Page Municipal Airport in northern Arizona. Not a lot of activity here in the middle of the night.

Not night, but early in the morning on ... Sunday.

Hard to keep up with times and days when she'd started in a different realm less than twenty-four hours ago, teleported to Atlanta, and now flew to Arizona.

Storm joined her and led them toward a man standing by a large black sport-utility vehicle like the executive car services at home. Storm caught her hand in his, a simple contact that always gave her a little unexpected happy feeling.

Illumination from the airport offered more than enough light for Evalle to see through her special sunglasses. Storm's natural night vision topped hers, but she believed he wore sunglasses to shield his eyes that sometimes glowed at an unexpected time.

Usually when someone had drawn his ire.

She needed eye protection for her sensitive vision and to shield her bright-nonhuman-green eyes from humans.

But wearing sunglasses at night around humans made her feel like some celebrity wannabe traveling incognito.

She'd hated the idea of flying out here until they were airborne, and she relaxed with Storm. He had a good idea about her meeting with the tribal seer.

Evalle would normally feel foolish making that request but leaving Atlanta had cut off her access to nonhuman friends. She had to find answers. Going to meet a Native seer might be a bust, but Evalle wouldn't discount a tribal member with powers.

It sounded as if Storm's father had been fairly powerful in his own right.

She hated living in limbo, not knowing definitively if she'd ever fully regain her powers or if her gryphon was gone forever.

No matter how hard she tried to accept that her beast wouldn't return, her heart pleaded to cling to the idea of shifting again.

Even if the news was bad, give her the known over the unknown any day.

Shaking off negative thoughts, she looked for the potential in a new approach. If the seer could pinpoint how Evalle's body lacked balance, that would be a start.

Fixing a problem began with understanding where to look.

Maybe someone here would surprise her and offer an insight others had missed.

"Thank you for coming out," Storm's uncle stepped forward with his hand extended, distracting Evalle from her thoughts. She compared him to the man whose face and body she knew so well.

His uncle shared the same teak skin tone and black hair as her mate though his uncle's had silver feathering his temples. She found the similarity in their faces more interesting. For the first time, she had an idea of what Storm's father might look like if he'd had a large frame with a little bulge of middle hidden beneath a nice-fitting dark suit.

She hadn't expected her first impression of him to be positive, but it was.

Storm shook hands and introduced her. "Bidziil, please meet Evalle, my mate."

His uncle offered her the same handshake, which she accepted with a smile, saying, "I'm sorry for the circumstances, but it's nice to meet you."

"It's nice to meet you, too." Then Bidziil turned to Storm. "I've arranged for private accommodations outside the casino, as you requested. I understand the intense noise and smells would disturb you, or ... would that be for *both* of you?"

Evalle picked up on a flash of irritation from Storm before he cleared up his uncle's confusion. "She's not a Skinwalker."

She gave Storm points for skipping over her identity without having to lie and pay a price physically.

Bidziil quickly added, "I only ask so that I can make your stay as comfortable as possible."

The negative energy dispersed then Storm moved on. "What's

going on out here?"

"There's a privacy window between the driver and the rear passenger area. I'll explain on the way."

"The way where?" Storm asked.

"A makeshift morgue at our law enforcement center."

Curiosity piqued, Evalle withheld questions to allow the uncle to explain.

Once they were moving, Bidziil explained about a dead tribal member named Sonny. Storm had to pick up how much Bidziil hurt for this young man, because Evalle could feel his pain.

After forty minutes of traveling south through dark roads with almost no highway lighting, they entered an area with streetlights. A six-story building stood as a centerpiece among mostly one-story structures. They passed a string of single-level buildings, which housed retail businesses and services from dentist offices to hair salons.

The driver pulled around to the back of what appeared to be a local police station with two cruisers, a truck, and sedan out front and a handful of private vehicles in back. He parked by a one-story dusty gray and brown building similar to other adobe structures she'd seen.

"We don't run a morgue here since our clan is too small to support one," Bidziil explained as they got out. "We needed a place to properly hold a body that's not buried immediately, so this is our holding facility."

Evalle and Storm met Bidziil at the rear of the vehicle where he cautioned, "Only a handful know about this death."

Bidziil had not told them everything about the body, claiming he didn't want to influence their first observations, but with no sign of foul play and no natural cause, it sounded like a suicide.

Why ask Storm to come out?

The more she listened to Storm's uncle, the more she picked up on his academic background. He appeared to be in his fifties and had the poise of a business professional.

On their way to the entrance, a man who appeared older than Bidziil and dressed in jeans with a belted buckskin top exited where a security guard stood next to the front door.

Some people wore a welcoming look in their eyes.

This man's gaze warned he shot trespassers.

Bidziil stopped abruptly and called to the man. "Why are you here, Nascha?"

The old guy didn't answer until he reached the three of them. "I am here to see that Bird Woman does not interfere."

"Haloke?" Storm's uncle asked. "Why would she come here? She hates this place."

"She thinks to know more than me."

Bidziil looked as if he might pop a vein. "That tells me nothing about why either of you would come here, Nascha. You hate this place, too. Wait, did you see Sonny's body?"

Medicine man lifted a bony chin at Bidziil. "I saw him. It's time to take the body far from here in the old way on a horse. Bury both before Bird Woman interferes."

Evalle asked Storm, "Is he talking about *killing* the horse?"

Storm said, "Yes. I'll explain later. Has to do with not wanting the spirit to return."

Her mate had sounded pained, which meant he wouldn't agree with harming an innocent animal.

Evalle shook her head. "How is that the horse's fault?"

Nascha must have caught their quiet exchange. He told Evalle in an angry voice, "Horse is honored."

"Bet the horse doesn't think so."

Squinting his wrinkled eyes, he ordered, "Who are you? Why do you wear dark glasses at night?"

Evalle had been sensing patience from Storm until Nascha demanded her identity.

Before she could reply, her mate leaned in and spoke in a tone that made it clear he wanted no one addressing her that way. "She is my mate. We prefer dark sunglasses during day and at night. That's all you need to know." Her mate pushed a load of power out with those words.

Eyes wide in shock, Nascha stepped back. His desire to ask who, or what, Storm was stood out on his face.

Grabbing his head, Bidziil grumbled, "I don't have the time or patience for this ongoing rift between you and Haloke."

Jerking back to face Bidziil, Nascha said, "She calls herself seer. How many times must I tell you she is not our seer?"

Bidziil snuck a glance at Storm as Nascha stopped glaring at her mate. It became clear to Evalle that Bidziil had intentionally diverted the old guy's attention from Storm and Evalle by bringing up the seer.

Waving a hand as if to be done with Nascha, Bidziil said, "Haloke is the best we've got. Everyone but *you* appreciates the time she spends with our people. She listens as much as she sees inside a person who is troubled, and you know she's given you good information on many."

Nascha harrumphed at that. "Not a healer."

Frankly, even though Evalle hadn't met the seer, she was already on Team Haloke.

"I didn't say she was, but she's been ours for years and still is," Bidziil snapped. "You don't like repeating yourself. Neither do I, but I seem to be doing more and more of it this past year. You need to let this go. There is no way I'll consider asking the elders to bring in another seer who *might* be stronger just because you don't like Haloke. You should appreciate that you had the benefit of training under a powerful medicine man while she had to scratch her own way."

"Bird Woman your fault."

"Fine." Bidziil sounded spent. "Would you at least give it a break for now so I can find out what happened to Sonny?"

Nascha got quiet, like a tornado waiting to explode. When he spoke, his words came out in condemnation. "You are blind with your eyes open."

As Nascha strode past Evalle, he tossed another glare at all of them.

She muttered, "What's that all about?" She caught herself. "Whoa. Sorry, Bidziil. That's none of my business."

Dismissing it, Bidziil said, "He says that to me all the time these days. Nothing we discussed is confidential. Everyone here has to put up with those two. They were tolerable until recent years. I don't know what happened, but I have bigger issues now. Sadly, they both mean well. I've seen Nascha spend days on end curing a child without taking a break to rest. He's a good man, but Haloke has given just as much even after the heartbreak she's suffered when she lost her son."

Seeming to brush off the friction, Bidziil led them to the door and spoke to the guard on his way into the morgue.

They crossed a tiny reception area to another door Storm held open. As Evalle followed Bidziil through, she caught a distinctive antiseptic tinge in the air and glanced at Storm.

He seemed unbothered by it in spite of his sharper senses.

Walking close behind, Storm asked his uncle, "What does Nascha have to say about Sonny's body?"

"Your father trained him, but he's not as gifted as Sani. No one I've ever met had his gifts. Anyhow, Nascha is pretty good otherwise, but he talks in riddles. All he said after I asked him about Sonny was 'dark spirits walk among us.'"

Evalle wanted to say, "That's a common occurrence in our world," but kept that to herself. Had the old guy meant it as information or a warning?

Instead she asked, "Is he really surprised to find spirits of any kind in a morgue?"

Bidziil lifted his arms in a frustrated motion. "I would think not. I'm only telling Storm what little I've gotten so far."

Storm asked, "And you're sure this can't be a homicide staged to throw you off the trail?"

"We're lucky to have someone who works as a registered nurse that's trained to be a medical examiner. He said he's never seen anything like it and found no evidence of drugs in the body, but he won't confirm the reason for death unless we allow an autopsy."

"Hold it." Evalle stopped walking. "You haven't autopsied the body yet?"

"No. He has no blood relation and I can't even share details with his friends until I know what happened," Bidziil explained. "We're calling this a suicide for now to minimize questions, though it pains me to say that about Sonny. No one wants to believe he'd take his own life." Storm's uncle seemed distracted for a moment, then shook it off and said, "Many of our people would be upset at an autopsy. We believe the spirit should be allowed to depart the body in a natural way where cutting a body open could actually lock the spirit to this plane."

"Thank you for explaining." Evalle appreciated how Bidziil hadn't held back when she asked anything. She glanced at Storm to see if she'd overstepped her place by questioning Bidziil.

Storm gave her a look of admiration, quieting any doubts.

Continuing with Evalle and Storm following, Bidziil reached the middle of a short hallway and stopped. "You'll see what I couldn't tell you over the phone. With all the high tech ways to listen to calls, I couldn't risk this getting out in the media, especially with rumors of preternatural beings in Atlanta in the news."

Evalle couldn't argue with that line of thinking if Sonny died by unnatural means, but did Bidziil think Storm was the only nonhuman in this world? Reporters and the Internet were ripping away the curtain of anonymity for their existence.

A waist-high solid wall with the same length of glass above it created one side of an all white and stainless-steel room.

Bidziil touched a button on an intercom unit mounted on the wide frame between the windows, then paused.

Turning to Evalle, he suggested, "You may not want to see this."

She politely assured him, "I've worked in a morgue. Not much surprises me."

Giving her a quick nod, Bidziil pushed the button and called out, "Henry?"

A young man in pale-blue scrubs that contrasted against his golden skin entered the enclosed room from a door on the far side. He wore his straight black hair cut in a short style.

Still pressing the button on the speaker, Bidziil said, "Please bring out Sonny's body."

Giving Storm's uncle a quick wave of acknowledgement, Henry reached for one of two drawers on the refrigeration unit and pulled out a gurney with a gray-skinned corpse.

Once Henry moved to where the three of them could view one side from head to toe, he waited for further instruction.

Evalle took a long look at the young man's body covered with smooth skin, which looked perfectly normal until she took in his face. She cringed at the disfigurement. Starting at the side of his cheek just below his eye, the skin had been gouged and ripped away from the tissue and bone underneath.

His fingernails were still gripping deep under the skin torn from his face. His neck remained in a rigid curve from straining in pain, thick muscles stood out from his throat and his mouth remained frozen in a silent scream of agony.

Had he done that damage to himself?

Evalle looked at Storm in horror but said nothing.

Storm had pulled his emotions in so tight she couldn't sense them, which told her this had to be hitting him hard enough he wanted to shield her from feeling it.

Storm asked, "Has anyone used chemicals on the body?"

"No. Again, that's why I wanted to get you here as quickly as possible. Sonny died just over twenty-four hours ago. He should be buried within four days, according to our beliefs. I'm hoping with your Skinwalker gifts you might pick up something beyond our abilities."

His uncle's frantic calls now made sense.

Bidziil reeked of misery, but he gathered himself to finish giving all he could. "We have no idea what happened, but there is nothing natural about that. I have to alert the tribe if we have a serial killer. If not, I still have to tell them if this means there's a threat of a different sort to our people. I asked the seer to contact the Holy People."

Storm whipped his head around to Bidziil. "That is not a door you should open."

Evalle watched the interplay. Why would Holy People be a problem?

Letting out a sigh born of exhaustion, Bidziil admitted, "I know. That's how desperate I was by the time I called you."

"Did your seer have anything to share?"

"Yes. The Holy People warned there would be more deaths unless I brought *you* here."

"They named Storm?" Evalle asked, no longer able to wait quietly.

Evidently Storm had the same question. "Are you sure they meant me?"

Bidziil explained how the spirits had actually referenced the son of the *old one*, who was of Bidziil's blood. He and the seer determined the Holy People had to mean Sani.

Evalle understood the point Bidziil was making but had to play devil's advocate when spirits were naming her mate. "*Old one* sounds like a term of respect for an elder. Are you sure they meant Storm's father?"

Storm answered her. "You're right about that term, but in this case the name Sani actually means *old one*."

"Exactly," Bidziil agreed. "We believe the Holy People sent us to find you."

Nodding, Storm said to Evalle, "Please wait here. I'm going to step inside and take a closer look at the body."

"Go ahead." She didn't envy him getting near that corpse with his heightened sense of smell.

Once he entered the room, Storm spoke to Henry, who backed away to the far wall. The guy sent a curious look to Bidziil, who lifted a finger, silently asking Henry to stand by.

Evidently, Henry was on the short list of people allowed to know about the condition of Sonny's body.

Storm walked around the gurney, studying the corpse closely as if looking for a mark or something that'd indicate why Sonny had died so viciously.

Once Storm had circled him, he stopped on the far side, allowing Evalle a clear view of her mate. Then he lifted both hands, palms down, holding them over Sonny's destroyed face.

Storm closed his eyes for a couple seconds.

He pulled his hands back and snapped his eyes open, staring down as if he'd seen something startling.

Backing up one step, he raised his arms again, but high above the body this time. He started chanting as he moved slowly around the gurney.

She couldn't hear the words, but she'd seen Storm in this mode before. If Bidziil opened a speaker, they'd hear the nasal sound of him speaking words learned from his father.

Evalle checked Henry to gauge a reaction from a member of the tribe.

At first, Henry appeared bored and impatient. He leaned against the wall with a bent knee.

As Storm continued his ritual, the body began to tremble.

Bidziil sucked in a breath and said, "I have to get Storm out of there."

Evalle said, "No. He knows what he's doing. If you interfere, you might harm Storm."

Bidziil gave her a weighty look.

She couldn't explain how she'd been through so many unusual situations with her mate and would know if he was in danger.

Small dark red patches started to appear across the chest, then down Sonny's leg. The patches spread like paint splattered on his skin. Once the blobs met, dark outlines formed around each splash of crimson color.

In seconds, the entire body had turned into one giant red patchwork.

The skin began cracking.

Storm's voice picked up volume, which happened when he pushed power into his chants.

Energy sizzled along the squiggly dark lines marking the outline of each red blob of skin.

The body lifted ten inches and floated. Those dark lines thickened and turned into a hard finish that reminded Evalle of a plastic shell.

The skin shattered.

Flames erupted along the outlines, shooting a foot high. It was as if someone had ignited Sonny's insides and the fire needed to escape.

Evalle checked on Henry again. His mouth flopped open and all color washed from his face.

Bidziil cursed and grabbed his hair. "Storm has to get out of there. I wouldn't forgive myself if he ends up hurt."

"Storm knows what he's doing," Evalle warned gently. "This is clearly a nonhuman issue, he can handle it." She never took her eyes off Storm and the smoldering corpse when she added, "However, if anything happens to him while we're here, you'll have more to worry about than a guilty conscience."

She felt Bidziil's eyes on her, probably wondering if she could back up her words.

Hurt Storm and there would be no question.

She'd given that warning as the woman who would not allow anyone to harm the man she loved and get away with it.

Bidziil made a sound like a pained moan.

She cut her eyes at him to see a glowing cloud engulf his body then slowly turn translucent until Bidziil stood there with his lips parted.

She put a hand on his arm. "Are you okay?"

Turning rounded eyes to her, he whispered, "I felt ... I can't describe it. Like Sonny's spirit hugged me."

She'd tell Storm about this later if Bidziil didn't, but for now she said, "It could have been him telling you goodbye."

Bidziil's pain eased for the moment. Now, she empathically

picked up awe and love from him.

Storm lowered his hands and studied the blackened corpse that had returned to lie upon the gurney. Next he spoke to the attendant, who refused to walk back over. Turning to the door, Storm stepped away and out to the hallway.

Bidziil shook his head and seemed to recover from his experience. He glanced at Evalle who just smiled at him.

No, she wouldn't share what he said. That had been a private moment. She was only glad it might have given Bidziil closure.

Turning to Storm, Bidziil asked, "Do you know what caused the death?"

"No."

Evalle gave Storm the question Bidziil should have asked. "What did you learn?"

Storm said, "Sonny's spirit was trapped. I released it and as the spirit escaped the body, it whispered to me."

Clearly not experienced with anything like this, Bidziil's eyes widened. "Wh-what did it say?"

"Something that sounded like *I see.*"

Evalle felt a chill race over her body.

His uncle had been right on two counts. That did not sound like a suicide or natural death. Storm had clearly come to the same conclusion.

Someone cast a spell or used dark majik on Sonny.

Evalle rubbed her arm, feeling an urge to wash her hands after being here. "Which way to the restroom?"

Bidziil led her to the ladies' room just off the reception area as he and Storm followed, discussing what they'd just learned.

Evalle's bootheels echoed over the bathroom tile, but she heard nothing else to indicate another person in the room. She washed and dried her hands, then finger-brushed her hair.

Seeing a black line exposed when she lifted her arms, she pulled the short sleeve up to show more skin.

Shit. She'd actually forgotten about the damn lines, veins or whatever they were, but they were getting longer and branching off more.

She let out a breath she'd been holding. Then she leaned into the mirror to take a closer look at the V opening of her buttoned shirt. Pulling it wide, she found another patch of jagged lines running down her breast. Maybe farther. No one seemed to be in here, so she unbuttoned her shirt fast to take a look.

The lines twisted almost like braids and ran across her abdomen as well as the long slash over her breast. She pulled up her jeans and found two new ones on her legs.

One thing for sure, what had started out as a spot on her arm was now spreading across her body faster.

If these had to do with leftover Noirre bleeding out of her, she'd probably be feeling the negative effects by now. The entire time she'd suffered with that nasty majik in her body, she'd battled preternatural creatures in Abandinu's realm while sick. She'd been unable to heal completely because the majik wouldn't allow her Belador blood to work with her Medb blood.

Nothing had prevented Garwyli or Storm from healing her, another indication she should have no Noirre in her system.

Also, Storm would have sensed the dark majik presence by now.

She ran through more possibilities, but finally admitted she was only dancing around the one she didn't want to accept.

These lines could be the definitive sign that her gryphon had been too damaged and would never recover.

CHAPTER 11

ON THE WAY OUT OF the morgue to their waiting car, Evalle struggled to dismiss her revelation in the bathroom.

There had to be a better explanation.

Her antagonistic conscience asked, *What else makes more sense?*

Evalle had no idea, but she'd been on the go nonstop from fighting Hoyt in Treoir to facing off with warlocks in Atlanta and now leaving a morgue in Arizona where something really bad had killed a young man.

Important life decisions shouldn't be made until she had a clear head.

Storm turned to her before they reached the car and asked, "All good?"

She heard the doubt in his voice, but still told him, "Yep. What about you?"

He put his arm around her shoulders and leaned closer. "I'm fine and I won't pester you every minute if you promise to come to me when you're ready to talk out what's bothering you."

Busted by the sexy lie detector.

"Fair enough." She snuggled her arm around his waist and gave him a squeeze to let him know she appreciated him not hounding her.

They made a short ride to the resort where the driver continued around the casino property until he reached the rear area. He parked next to a walkway surrounded by desert landscaping that belonged in a style magazine.

A thick slab of gray stone made into a sign indicated the direction of private villas down the natural walkway. Storm would avoid staying in the casino hotel for many reasons but had given his uncle two that hadn't been insulting.

Bidziil stepped out and told the driver to stay put, that he'd handle the bags. He met Storm at the rear cargo area.

Storm lifted both bags with a simple, "We won't need any help."

Keeping his voice down, Bidziil asked, "Have you come up with any ideas?"

Evalle stepped away to give the men a moment to talk. Even with her Belador powers not back to full capacity, she could hear everything in the quiet night.

Storm lowered the bags to the ground. "I don't want to point a finger at anyone until I know more, but what happened to Sonny wasn't a simple spell."

"A spell? This majik stuff is over my pay grade," Bidziil mumbled. "What do we do next?"

Storm hesitated for a brief moment. "No one is going to like this, but you have to determine if anyone in the tribe is performing dark majik."

Bidziil pulled back and scratched his neck. "I've never heard of anyone doing that in our clan."

"I'm not surprised, because no one who does will advertise it," Storm contended. "I'd like to get the security people you trust in one room and question them, then suggest things to watch for while in the community. They may have seen or heard something they didn't realize was odd."

Bidziil said, "I don't want to sound close-minded, but Sonny would never have been involved in any dark majik stuff. He didn't do drugs, didn't drink, didn't gamble ... hell, he didn't really date much, because he was so driven to succeed."

"If that was a dark majik spell, Sonny might have done nothing worse than being in the wrong place at the wrong time."

Evalle admired her mate's soothing voice. Storm had issues with his uncle, but that hadn't stopped him from offering comfort.

Bidziil stared off with pinched mouth and a gaze full of disappointment. He wiped a sleeve over his damp eyes and swallowed. "It might sound crazy, but I ... I could swear I felt his spirit leave tonight. I hope so. I need to know he's at peace."

Storm spoke with confidence. "He is."

Standing straighter, Bidziil sounded more like a strong businessman. "Thank you for what you did. His death is killing me, but seeing him like that and now knowing someone really might have done that to him ... I will do anything and give you any resources to find them, but I have no idea where to start looking for dark majik."

Storm consoled, "I understand, but I do have the skills and gifts to figure it out. Also, I'm the most objective person here, because I have no connection to anyone. That means you'll have to be open-minded as we narrow down potential suspects among your clan."

"How are we going to get someone to admit to being a ... " Bidziil seemed at a loss for the right word.

"Witch," Evalle supplied, stepping over to enter the conversation, but keeping her comments just as quiet. "Lucky for you one of Storm's gifts as a Skinwalker is his ability to tell if anyone is lying."

For that, she earned a glance from Storm followed by a wave of love that brushed her empathic sense.

"No kidding?" Bidziil seemed more impressed than shocked. "That could wrap this up quickly if we can find suspects."

"Possibly," Storm allowed. "After I meet with your security people, we'll narrow the field by striking the easy names off the list starting with people like Nascha and Haloke."

Bidziil groaned. "Nascha will lose his mind if he realizes he's suspected of using dark majik. Haloke will, too."

"I don't really suspect your healers, but that doesn't mean they haven't been around someone learning from either of them that they turned away out of instinct."

"Huh. I hadn't thought of that, Storm. Nascha has spent time teaching others how to use their inner strength to heal themselves, which he says is giving him a look at potential future medicine men, or women," Bidziil added with a little smile in Evalle's direction.

Storm cautioned, "For now, let's not allow anyone to realize they're on the list, including Nascha and Haloke. That way, everyone will continue in their natural manner."

Sounding relieved, Bidziil said, "Thank you. This will go faster if I don't have to waste time pacifying those two."

"I don't want to upset the clan either," Storm said then brought up something new. "By the way, I'd like our own car. We don't have drivers at home, and I prefer the freedom to come and go as needed. I'm sure I can find my way around."

Stretching his neck, Bidziil stifled a yawn. "I'll have one delivered to the parking space across the street."

Evalle looked past him to where three vehicles sat in a paved lot.

Bidziil pointed toward a string of six attractive adobe-style structures dotting the curved path leading away from where they stood. He offered a business card to Evalle and told them, "That has the code to open the third villa. You'll see the image of a gecko carved into the door. My contact information is on the flipside."

Evalle thanked him and made a mental note of the code. Storm would carry the bags, which left her to unlock the door.

"You can have anything you need delivered," Bidziil went on explaining. "We assign a staff member to each villa, so you have someone who becomes quickly familiar with your needs. When I assigned this unit and said no casino staff member was to visit without my approval, one of the young women working her way up the administrative side stepped up. She volunteered to be your rep to free me up from having to approve others."

Evalle kept catching the way this man spoke about his young people. She commented, "Sounds like you have a competent staff."

Bidziil gave a sad smile. "That's the team attitude we work to foster among the young talent joining our organization. Adsila will deliver the keys for your vehicle in the next half hour unless that's too late for you."

"No, we normally operate at night," Storm replied, making it clear they ran on their own schedule. "If anything new comes up, let me know. I'm willing to meet whenever you call your people in."

His uncle sounded a little recharged. "I'm headed back to my office to check the schedule and see if the top level of my security team is available. I'll let you know as soon as I bring them in."

"Sounds good."

When Storm turned to leave, Bidziil said, "Thank you both for coming out. I know you don't think these are your people, Storm, but they'd welcome you the minute they know you're Sani's son. Many remember your father."

Turning back, Storm gave a curt, "You're welcome." Then he asked, "Do *you* remember my father?"

Evalle cringed a little at the censure in Storm's tone after these two seemed to be getting along, but he'd made it clear to her that he held his uncle's ambitious plans responsible for the rift between brothers.

Holding Storm's gaze for a long time, Bidziil said in a wistful voice, "Yes, I do remember Sani, but mostly from when we were kids and as close as two brothers could be. For the record, I regret being an idiot when Sani left. We were young, passionate, and headstrong. Ten years later, I'd have handled our last meeting differently."

Evalle watched the byplay, fascinated at seeing this sliver of Storm's history. Would his uncle's admission open a door to allow these men at least a distant connection?

Storm's jaw muscle tensed. "It's been thirty years. Why didn't you reach out to him in all that time?"

"I did."

"What?" Storm asked too quickly to hide his shock.

Anger and disbelief spun off her mate in a flash wave, but that reaction meant Bidziil hadn't lied, or Storm would have called him on it.

Evalle wished Bidziil had waited to start this conversation at a better time than when they all stood in a parking lot.

His uncle said, "I wrote letters. Sani called a few times. Our worlds were so far apart, but I offered to come see him. I asked again to see *both* of you when he told me you were born, but Sani said no, that he didn't want me to get hurt in the jungle. Why he thought I couldn't visit safely, I have no idea."

Evalle had a pretty good idea after meeting Storm's evil mother, the Ashaninka witch doctor. Sani might have been a strong medicine man, but he hadn't possessed Storm's ability to detect her darkness or a threat to him and his child until too late.

In the next moment, Storm's anger backed down then shifted into frustration. "I know why my father said not to and he was right, but I don't want to get into that discussion."

Bidziil lifted a hand. "I understand. I just wanted you to know I did care and still do."

When the silence turned brittle, Evalle asked, "Would you two like to talk at our unit?"

Storm said nothing.

She took that as a no.

His uncle gave her a warm smile. "That's kind of you, Evalle. I'd like to talk more, but there will be time after we get this nasty majik business sorted out. I just wanted Storm to know I do regret the mistakes I made thirty years ago." Bidziil gave Storm a tentative look, one that suggested maybe—just maybe—things could be different.

Storm said nothing one way or another.

Stepping around to open his car door, Bidziil said, "Don't hesitate to call for anything. Talk to you both later."

His uncle got in and the car drove off.

Storm watched until it vanished around the end of the tall casino building, then turned to the path with a long sigh.

Evalle fell into step and walked along quietly at first then had to get something off her chest. "Sorry if I put you on the spot back there by asking him to our villa."

"You didn't. I just ... don't know what to say to that man. I've been angry at him for a long time."

"Since your dad died?"

Carrying the bags with little effort, Storm walked a few steps before answering. "Pretty much. Guess I wanted to blame everyone when he died, but the witch doctor was the only one responsible for killing him."

Evalle agreed a hundred percent after battling the crazy woman. "Does Bidziil know exactly what happened to your father?"

"No. As you can tell by his reactions tonight, I've told him little about myself and our life with the Ashaninka."

"He sounded ... sincere."

"I know," Storm said as if he'd just admitted a major sin.

She laughed. "Why did that come out so glum?"

He gave her a half-hearted smile. "Hearing his words makes it hard to hold onto a grudge I've nurtured for a long time. Makes me feel like a jerk for all the negative thoughts I've had about him."

She leaned over and kissed her mate.

Storm cocked an eyebrow at her. "Not that I'm complaining, but what was that for?"

Hoping to lift his spirits, Evalle said, "To let you know you're not one. I wouldn't be kissing you if you were."

Storm's eyes darkened at that. "When I can unload this luggage, I'll give you a proper thank-you kiss."

She no longer felt mixed emotions pouring off him, which hopefully meant he'd settled on being at peace for now. Thinking about Sonny, she asked, "Who would be performing dark majik here? Does the tribe have covens?"

"No. At least, not normally. The tribe my father told me of does not support dark majik. I have to disagree with Bidziil on one point. These people may have cared for Sani, but they wouldn't welcome me. The clan wouldn't be happy to find a Skinwalker among them, which is synonymous with witch."

"Wait, do they think all *witches* are bad, that there's no distinction between light and dark?"

"Many do, but keep in mind I'm only speaking based on what my father shared about this clan. Still, I don't think it's much different in other tribal communities. They believe a witch can take the form of an animal and perform majik, thus the tie to a Skinwalker. If not, he or she would be a shaman or medicine man expected to heal the tribe."

She didn't like that Storm wouldn't be accepted here, but she understood. Every culture had its beliefs.

Plus, Storm would point out that he was, after all, of demon blood. She'd remind him that small part had been buried beneath all the good.

Storm continued, "I'm sure there's more to their belief than what little I can tell you and things could've changed in all the years since my father lived here, but he spoke of customs passed down from one generation to the next. He said that while some had lost their way with drugs, alcohol, and other temptations, the majority of the Dine were peaceful people with good hearts."

While listening, she noted the emblem on each door. The first two buildings had a wolf and a bird that might be a roadrunner.

The third southwestern-style villa painted an inviting sand color had a lizard image carved into the door.

"Is that a gecko?" she asked.

Storm slowed his stride and looked over. "Yes. The gecko, or Brother Lizard as it is also called, is considered by some a symbol of dreams and others a symbol of protection."

She liked how Storm shared little details without her asking, as if maybe just being here touched a place inside him. Reaching the door first, she punched numbers into a keypad lock and heard it snick open.

Pushing the door open, she stepped into a stunning interior with terra-cotta floors that gave way to hardwood in an open floor plan. The place smelled of new leather and fresh paint. Cream-colored walls had been formed with soft corners around a fireplace and with shelves sculpted as part of the entire structure. All of it gave off a peaceful feeling with a sofa upholstered in tooled leather and a coffee table with a rich wood finish. Rugs appeared to be wool woven with geometric designs.

Everything about this villa had a fresh and welcoming appeal.

Storm walked past her, then paused as he swept a look around to the dining area between the great room and kitchen. With a glance at the stairway with an ornate black wrought-iron handrail, he said, "Looks like the master bedroom is up there."

Evalle hurried upstairs behind him and into the bedroom where a light-colored wood covered the wall behind a large bed on four thick legs. Each piece of wood furniture had a custom feel.

He sat the bags down and crossed the space to check the window decorated with beautifully woven curtains one would expect in Arizona.

Turning back, he sounded relieved. "I asked for blackout shades that permitted no light to enter."

"And they just ran out to get those?" She laughed. "I haven't seen any major box store." Who asked for specific window coverings?

Not that she didn't appreciate Storm's thoughtfulness with her lethal reaction to the sun.

Storm walked over to her. "You won't see major department stores unless you go to the cities, sweetheart. Big-box stores would crush the Native-operated businesses. Casinos are normally very accommodating. The shades I asked for were nothing compared to what a high-rolling gambler would demand." He cupped a hand around her neck and leaned down to kiss her ... and kiss her.

She wrapped her arms around him, forgetting everything except being with Storm. He hooked her waist with an arm, pulling her close then ran his hand from her neck to cup her breast.

Oh, yes. She gripped his hair and pulled him deeper into the kiss. His thumb brushed over her nipple pushing against her thin bra and shirt.

His lips slowed until he gave her a soft finish. "Mercy."

He kissed her neck. "One of these days, it's just going to be you, me, and ... "

She mumbled, "A night alone."

"No. A tent."

She groaned.

He laughed. "You can't get any more alone than out in the middle of nowhere in a tent."

Stepping back, she shook her head. "I want air conditioning and showers. In fact, I want that shower right now."

Chuckling, he lifted her bag and placed it on a suitcase stand then dropped his duffel beside it.

As she dug out fresh clothes, Storm announced, "Go ahead. I want to see what we have to eat and drink before that woman arrives with the keys. That way I can tell her if we need anything now."

"Good thinking." With everything she needed in hand, Evalle stepped into the bathroom. Her gaze went to the mirror as she emptied her pockets on the counter and unbuttoned her shirt.

Storm wouldn't be happy when he saw the lines crawling across her body. He'd have to wait until she finished showering to talk about it if she couldn't put it off until tomorrow.

He'd fall back on the only option he could offer ... to bond with her.

Would that fix this problem?

No one knew. Also, hurrying to perform the ceremony just to give her more power with no guarantee of her healing seemed to ruin the beauty of the true reason behind bonding.

Plus, what if bonding didn't fix her problem?

She would have tied Storm's energy to her corrupted power eternally.

The word eternal scared her when she thought what it would mean for Storm.

The doorbell dinged.

Evalle buttoned her shirt quickly and backtracked from the bathroom to the top landing where she had a view of the door.

This might only be about delivering the keys to their car. But if Bidziil needed her, she didn't have time to shower.

Storm opened the door to a twentyish woman who shared his skin tone, black hair, and sharp cheekbones of many Native people. Her beige blazer sported a distinctive tribal design on the cuff and dark pants with stylish boots. She had gray eyes instead of brown and her smile of straight teeth bumped up what would have been an average face to attractive.

"Good evening, Mr. Tso. I'm Adsila. Our Mr. Tso asked that I deliver your car. It's a maroon Yukon parked in the private lot for these units. I'll be happy to show you where that is. Here are your keys."

Accepting them, Storm said, "Thank you. Your boss pointed out the lot."

When the young woman smiled again, Evalle felt for her.

The smile lacked any joy. Her facial muscles were probably on auto-drive by this time of night if she worked in the casino offices and had been up all day. Bidziil had spoken as if she'd agreed to be the go-to person for this villa in addition to her standard duties.

Bidziil had to be doing something right to garner that level of commitment to a job.

"You're welcome," Adsila said. "Is there anything else I can bring you and ... " The woman's gaze lifted to Evalle. "Your wife?"

Storm told her, "No, thanks. We're good."

With her smile still in place, the woman said, "Very good. Just call the front desk and they'll find me immediately if you do require anything additional. Also, Mr. Tso asked that you give him a call."

Storm tipped her and closed the door as she stepped away. Looking at Evalle, he said, "Give me a minute to call my uncle."

Evalle had been right to hold off showering.

When Storm finished the brief conversation, he gave her the bottom line. "Bidziil has three security people he'd like me to meet. Do you want to go?"

The shower called to her plus she could think of nothing her presence would add to the meeting. Maybe Storm and his uncle would talk some more about Storm's dad if left alone.

"If you need me, I'll be happy to go, but if I'll just be standing around I'd rather take a hot shower and get out of these clothes."

Storm waved her off. "That's fine. Stay here. I'll be surprised if anything comes of this. I'm hoping to give them signs of what to look for like unusual animal deaths from someone experimenting before attempting to work on a human."

"You think this is a novice?"

He had a thoughtful expression. "It's hard to say. The spell was significant, but Bidziil would know if anyone new had settled here. This is like a small town where everyone knows everyone and should notice anything odd if a tribal member has gotten into dark majik recently. If this is the first time practicing on a person, there may be instances of animal deaths ignored as not worth mentioning."

"That makes sense." She said, "Be careful. Love you."

He winked. "I will. Love you more."

Once he closed the door and the lock clicked, she hurried to the bathroom. Not as huge as the one they had at home, but nicely appointed. Flipping buttons on her shirt, she shed all of her clothes.

Her hands shook with panic.

No, no, no.

More lines had appeared even from when she'd checked in the morgue bathroom. Why? One patch ran down the inside of her thigh and a new one crossed her abdomen.

This might be a mistake, but she wanted to see if her touch would make them extend again. She placed her finger on a line that started across her abdomen.

Three dissected from the central vein and continued two inches.

No touching the artwork. She yanked her hand back. Her stomach roiled with sick fear.

Grabbing a towel, she tried to block the lines from view, but the wrap couldn't cover her entire body.

How much worse would this be by morning?

CHAPTER 12

A LONG HOT SHOWER SOUNDED WONDERFUL, but Evalle dashed through a fast one instead and dressed in record time. The central air-conditioning ran, giving the villa a nice chill. Great for sleeping, but she exchanged her nightshirt for one of Storm's long-sleeved T-shirts that fell halfway down her thighs.

That covered more skin, too.

Plus, Storm liked when she wore his clothes.

Now to ask someone to go hunting for her.

Snagging her mobile phone off the dresser, she crawled onto the bed, piled pillows to lean against, and pulled the cover across her bare legs.

Her body practically sighed at being horizontal.

Normally she wouldn't text anyone this time of night with it closing in on two in the morning in Atlanta, but she'd really like to talk to Adrianna.

Hopefully her friend wouldn't smack her long distance with a shot of Witchlock for waking her up.

Adrianna's reply text read: *Yes, I'll talk, but not until I have tea in hand. Sit tight.*

Evalle answered on the first ring. "Sorry. I know it's late."

"I wasn't sleeping that well anyhow," Adrianna said, sounding half awake.

"Why not?"

"Stupid reason," Adrianna groused, noncommittal.

Evalle thought about what the culprit could be. "Stupid *man* reason, witch?" Had Adrianna returned to Atlanta with Evalle and Storm so she could check on Isak and Kit, two humans who knew about preternaturals?

One of which happened to be the idiot male Adrianna had been involved with for a short time.

"Everything does not involve Isak, *gryphon*," Adrianna answered in a teasing tone. Then she gasped. "Oh shit, Evalle, I didn't mean to say that."

They referred to each other as witch and gryphon all the time. Evalle didn't want to lose the easy way she and Adrianna had always communicated.

She assured her friend, "It's okay, Adrianna. You're one of the few people not treating me like a piece of china. Besides, it was funny to hear you curse."

"I'm liable to say anything when I'm not fully awake, but the tea will kick in soon. Speaking of your gryphon, how are you doing?"

See? Adrianna didn't dance around any topic. Evalle leaned back against the fluffy pillows and looked out at the clear black sky beyond the wide windows where stars twinkled. "That's kind of why I wanted to talk."

"Did something happen?" the witch asked cautiously.

"Before we left for Arizona, I—"

"Wait. What? You're in Arizona? Why in the world are you and Storm there?"

Evalle filled in Adrianna on what they were doing because she had zero doubt Storm would tell their friend. With that explained, Evalle said, "So back to why I texted. I have more of those strange jagged lines on my body. I'm dreading going to sleep and waking up to a new surprise. I'm hoping you can find out something for me."

"Have you shown them to Storm?" Adrianna sounded as if she had more to say but was holding back.

"Yes, back at Treoir. But I haven't shown him the new spread yet. He left before I took a shower. To be honest, I wanted to talk to you first. Storm has enough on him."

"He won't feel burdened," Adrianna said quietly.

Evalle admitted what she hadn't shared with anyone. "I know he'll never show any sign of the strain this is putting on him, but we both know he's really stressed over my missing gryphon. Also, I'm tired of him constantly thinking I'm going to die. He unloaded all his healing power on me. What else can he do? Well, we can always bond if I run out of options, but that worries me, too."

When Adrianna said nothing, Evalle took that as agreeing with her points and continued. "I don't want to be a nonstop repair project for him. So back to the lines. Can you find out anything?"

"I actually do know something." Adrianna had spoken too quietly. She didn't sound excited as if she had good news.

"And?" Evalle prodded.

"I started researching as soon as I got home from Treoir. I'm not going to waste our time going through how I got this, but I tapped someone connected to the Sterling witches."

Evalle's heart fell.

Adrianna had been born a Sterling witch, but turned her back on her family when they basically sold her twin sister to a crazy witch who cooked her majik.

For Adrianna to contact anyone associated with them was ... hard to put into words.

Swallowing, Evalle said, "I'm sorry to have put you in that position."

"You didn't. I'm a big girl. I made the decision."

"Still, it means more than you know that you'd do that. Thank you."

"You're welcome, Evalle, but you may not like what I found out."

Preparing for whatever Adrianna had discovered, Evalle said, "Lay it on me."

The witch hesitated then said, "The bottom line is a mage placed a spell on two different nonhumans, which resulted in similar lines crawling across the bodies until they covered the skin completely."

"What happened then?" Evalle closed her eyes at the heartbreak in Adrianna's voice. At least her friend would give her a straight answer.

"When the lines joined, they began tightening until they cut through the body, killing both test examples."

Evalle opened her eyes and lifted her arm, staring at the inky lines. As an afterthought, she asked, "What kind of nonhumans did the mage put the spell on?"

"Oh, Evalle, that's what I hate to tell you." Adrianna's soft breathing filled the line for a couple seconds. "He used demons.

Those lines might be something left from the spell the mage placed on you in Abandinu."

Evalle barely listened after the word demons.

Her heartbeat pounded in her ears.

She now felt robbed after all the time she'd delayed bonding with Storm. In her foolish heart, she'd always thought she could fix her body then join with him in a special ceremony.

Unless some miracle cure happened, which didn't sound likely if these lines resulted from the mage's spell, she could not allow Storm to bond with her.

Ever.

Neither could she tell him what she'd just learned.

Not after she'd given him permission to activate the bond at any moment if she got into dire straits.

She had to breathe in and out, in and out, forcing a calm over her body she didn't feel. When she could say the words without her voice cracking, Evalle said, "Thank you, Adrianna."

"I'm sorry, Evalle. I wanted to give you good news when I saw you."

"Me, too." She struggled against the pain spearing her. Being found and rescued from Abandinu's realm had been incredible. Tristan bringing her back to life ranked up there with a true miracle.

All that for naught.

"Do you want me to come out there and give Witchlock a try, Evalle? We should be able to find somewhere away from any people in a land that wide-open to experiment."

Evalle started to laugh, but it wouldn't have sounded happy. Twisting the tail of Storm's shirt into a knot, she said, "Thanks, but no."

"Why not?"

"I gave my word to Storm I wouldn't let you try unless we bonded first."

Adrianna cursed again, a record for her. "You don't think he'd change his mind with this news?"

"No, and I don't want you to tell him. Nothing would stop him from joining his power to mine if he knew. Not that I have much left, because I lose more as I gain new lines."

How could it end this way? Evalle couldn't muster the fighting spirit she'd had until now.

"Listen, Evalle, whatever the mage did to that demon doesn't mean your lines will kill you."

"You don't have to keep reassuring me," Evalle said, though Storm would have heard the lie in her voice. "I said I wanted the truth and I appreciate it. I really do."

Angry now, Adrianna grumbled, "Maybe this has nothing to do with the mage and the lines are a sign your gryphon is trying to break out."

"You think my beast is trying to *hatch* out of my skin?" Evalle asked with a little of her normal sarcasm. "How is that a good idea?"

"I don't know," Adrianna crabbed. "I'm brainstorming. Work with me. I hate having no plan of attack and no idea what we're fighting."

"Welcome to my world." Evalle appreciated Adrianna's fury on her part. She didn't want to leave her friend feeling all was lost. It might just be later on, but at the moment Evalle had to find her backbone. She still lived to fight tomorrow.

Determined to keep a strong front for her friend, she said, "Don't despair, witch. I do have a plan."

"Oh?" Adrianna perked up. "What is it?"

"Storm is getting me an invitation to meet the tribal seer. According to him, members of the tribe meet with her, then she figures out what's wrong with their body. They take that diagnosis to their medicine man who heals them."

"And you don't think the seer will figure out you're nonhuman?" the witch asked in a doubtful voice.

"I hope not. They aren't big on Skinwalkers out here. His uncle knows Storm is one and a guy at the morgue had a demonstration of Storm's majik, but Storm chanted when he used his majik so the guy probably thinks he's a medicine doctor. I don't think I have to bare my soul to the seer, just ask what she sees out of balance with my Hózhó."

"Your what? Is that what they call a gryphon in their language?" Adrianna teased, probably doing all she could to lighten the mood.

Evalle smiled in spite of her heavy heart. She tried explaining something she had no true understanding about. "No. I can't let anyone know I'm not human or that pretty much blows Storm's cover. Hózhó is about a person's energy. She sees what's out of whack with a body's harmony or something. I don't know if it will work since I'm neither human nor a tribal member, but I'm open to anything at this point."

Rustling of Adrianna moving around came through the lines. "Sure you don't want me to just be there during the day when you can't go out in the sun?"

Life had changed greatly since gaining friends.

Adrianna, in particular, had turned into one of the best.

"Thanks for the offer, but Storm has cloaked a vehicle for us. I'm fine. I'll let you know when we get back to Atlanta."

"Call me anytime." Then Adrianna was gone.

After finishing the call, Evalle studied the inky-looking lines for the longest time. She wanted to tell Storm what she'd learned. Wanted him to wrap her up and tell her they'd beat this.

But that would be selfish and dangerous.

He would bond immediately, even knowing it might kill him.

Nope. She would protect him this time.

The lines covered maybe twenty percent of her body, which meant she didn't have to face him yet.

She stalked around the room, bored and restless when she'd expected to be ready to sleep. Changing direction, she went downstairs to the great room but dismissed watching the television. She hated to figure out a new remote control.

Had Storm's uncle put blackout shades on the glass sliding door at the end of the room?

She strolled over to discover this room would be just as light-proof.

Finding the latch release, she opened the glass door and stepped out to a private patio complete with a fire pit surrounded by outdoor furniture. An interesting assortment of desert plants filled containers of all shapes and sizes.

Had the local members made those clay pots?

A half wall matching the house design and color enclosed the space on three sides with a wrought-iron gate exit that lead to the casino hotel and pool area thirty yards away.

She found a lounger and stretched out in it to stare at a star-filled sky she never saw in the city.

Maybe Storm had a point about camping some time if she

survived this. She wasn't ready to give up him or Feenix. Or her friends. Damn. Her heart ached as if she'd been stabbed.

If she didn't calm down by the time Storm returned, he'd know something was up immediately.

Slowly, she relaxed and let her eyelids flutter shut.

Flapping reached her ears, waking her.

She forced her heavy eyes open.

A large bird swooped by overhead, then was gone. She hadn't brought her sunglasses down, but no one would see her in the enclosure.

Leaning back, she drifted off again, missing her gryphon. Life sucked.

She wanted the life she'd had, warts and all, before she'd been snatched from Atlanta.

Flapping started again.

She blinked, seeing a large dark bird with a white head come flying down and land on the short wall next to the gate fifteen feet away.

An eagle?

She rubbed her eyes and looked again.

Yep. How fun was that?

The bird sat still and stared straight ahead, paying her little attention.

She opened her senses to it and got ... nothing.

Well, hell. Was she losing her empathic ability now?

She stayed parked on the lounger. At one time, she'd have had confidence in protecting herself from any creature. Not so much these days, but she wouldn't harm an eagle or any other natural animal that didn't try to kill her.

The eagle stood an easy three feet tall. It perched with moonlight shining on its back, leaving the bird in silhouette.

Evalle's natural night vision had always been crisp, especially when she went without sunglasses. This might be how humans saw. With the bird's back to the light, all she could see on the glowing white head were two black spots for eyes.

Speaking softly so as not to disturb it, she said, "Hey there."

Slowly, the bird angled its head until the beak pointed in her direction.

What was it about a wild animal or bird that made a person

want to pet it?

She had the urge to stroke the feathers, but while that beak might not be as large as the one on her gryphon, it could snap the bones in her hand.

A deep longing for her gryphon hit her again.

Do something, anything, to avoid thinking about it, she coached herself.

Not moving a muscle, they stared at each other for what felt like ten minutes.

When she realized it intended to stay, she leaned back, relaxed. "I envy you. I'll never shift into a gryphon and fly high above the land again."

The eagle angled its head in a pose of curiosity.

"You don't believe me?" She shrugged. "I did shift at one time, but someone wrecked my body. Now I can't even feel my beast any more."

The eagle showed no sympathy. No reaction at all.

Fair enough. She didn't want to be pitied.

Not even by a bird.

Sure, she probably looked stupid talking to a bird, but people told their dogs and cats everything and she needed a friend right now. One she wouldn't be burdening.

A noise pulled her attention away from her friend.

Evalle lifted up, looking over the wall, but the villas on each side were dark and silent as if vacant.

After a minute, she eased back down, glad the eagle hadn't spooked.

She needed a little company, especially after Adrianna's call.

Breathing deeply in and out, the tension slipped from her body. The bird had a calming presence. It didn't care who she was or that she couldn't fly. It seemed content to spend this time just being.

That sounded like a sound idea to try.

To be honest, just being able to talk about what bothered her helped, especially the things she couldn't tell Storm. "Are you mated?"

Stern silence answered her.

Huh, maybe the eagle had a sad story of its own.

Stretching her arms, she crossed them behind her head. "You

don't want to talk about it. I get it, but I could use some advice. I was ready to bond with my mate before I got kidnapped then I put it off. He understands, especially about me losing my gryphon, because he's got a jaguar inside him." She longed for the future they should have. "We made a great pair of shifters, but bonding is off the table now."

The eagle remained in its regal pose, patient as a statue as she unloaded some of the crap on her chest.

More people should listen the way this bird did.

She lay there, watching the eagle for the longest time until her eyelids became heavy again.

The world spun slowly. She floated in gray nothing.

Then clouds in the sky passed by ... no, *she* passed the clouds.

She was flying.

Wind brushed over her face as she soared high above the ground. A dark-eyed eagle appeared thirty feet away keeping pace with her. No problems existed among the clouds. Nothing could touch her this far above the world.

She lost track of time, content to glide back and forth.

A sharp sound woke her.

She jerked awake and pushed up on one arm, looking around the room in total darkness.

The bedroom?

Hadn't she been on the patio?

What was she doing upstairs? Shoving hair off her face, she muttered, "Damn, am I sleepwalking now?" She hoped not. "What a weird dream."

Footsteps tapping on the staircase grew closer. The sound that woke her could've been the door opening downstairs.

Evalle stilled, waiting.

Storm entered the room but didn't turn on the lights. He took care not to blind her. Were her eyes still sensitive? Good thing she'd ended up inside. What if she'd slept until sunrise on the patio?

He started undressing. "Did you sleep?"

"I nodded off long enough to have a strange dream."

"Might be the gecko influence," he teased.

That didn't actually comfort her. "How'd your meeting go?"

"I asked the security team about anything unusual that might've happened recently or the past year. No one had anything to report, but I spent time describing potential signs of strange activity. Now they know what to look for and are going into the community to do some quiet snooping, which I can't."

"What about the seer?"

Storm yawned. "I'm sorry. I didn't get a chance to bring it up tonight. There were too many people around and I didn't want to put Bidziil on the spot when he had an audience. Before we finished the meeting, he got called to handle a situation with an important casino customer. I let him go, but I haven't forgotten."

"No big deal." She tried to squash her panic at feeling time running out.

He climbed into bed and pulled her back against his body, cocooning her in his heat. Nuzzling her hair aside so he could kiss her neck, he said, "That almost sounded like a white lie. Getting you set up with the seer *is* a big deal to me. I will definitely handle it tomorrow."

"Thank you." She did her best to shake off her stress and settle into his embrace. Having him close helped. A lot.

The dream about the eagle still bothered her, though. She asked, "Does the eagle have meaning out here, you know, like the gecko is about dreams?"

Draping his arm over her waist, he yawned ending in a growl, then said, "Yes, they're sacred."

"I know eagles are protected."

"No, I mean they're sacred to the Dine," he corrected, then couldn't stifle another yawn. "In fact, their feathers are sought after by Natives to use for different reasons, including something good like a celebration. People in other countries pay a fortune for them. The federal government has stiff penalties, which is good, but that also created problems on reservations in the past."

"Why?"

"If a medicine man wanted feathers for a ceremony or healing, it meant applying to the wildlife authorities. I think they may have fixed that issue, but I'd have to ask Bidziil. Why the interest in eagles?"

"I was on the patio tonight, just looking at stars, and one landed on the wall."

"No kidding? You should feel honored. That seems unusual

for it to land so close to the ground if it wasn't hunting, not to mention being near a person."

She *had* gone to the patio tonight, hadn't she?

An eagle landed there, right?

Storm's fingers had been stroking her skin, but the motion slowed until they stilled, and his breathing evened out.

Or had she fallen asleep and dreamed it all?

A sick feeling washed over her.

Could she be hallucinating on top of everything else?

She curled against his shoulder, trying to understand what was happening. Was the dream or hallucination related to her black lines?

Lifting an arm, she squinted to see if they'd traveled any farther.

She didn't have to look far.

Her hand was covered.

CHAPTER 13

WHERE'S EVALLE?
She needs us.
His jaguar raced into the dark night, eating up miles. Not fast enough.
Keep running.
His animal caught her scent.
There. He could see her. He couldn't shout in this form. He shifted back and kept running on two feet. "Evalle!"
The harder he ran, the further away she got.
Evalle turned and smiled at him ... then her body yanked backwards. Terrified screams shook the air. Use majik. Don't lose her. Black wind tore at his skin. His nose and ears bled.
Her screams spiraled into silence.
He couldn't hear her.
Could. Not. See. Her!
Nooo!

Storm woke with a start, sweating and panting. He stared at the blacked-out windows in the dark bedroom, waiting for his heart to slow down. His jaguar vibrated inside him, pushing to get out. He reached around the bed ...

No Evalle.

He could hear the shower going. She was in the villa. He dropped his head into his hands. Dreams were sometimes just a mash of what happened in life. Other times they had meaning. The one he'd just had felt heavy with meaning.

Claws broke through his fingers.

He forced the jaguar to back down.

The dream must have rattled his animal.

Why was Evalle up before him? She was a snuggler. Liked it when he stayed in bed to play. Had she not slept well? The illuminated clock on the nightstand confirmed it was after eleven. Late in the morning for day-workers, but he and Evalle normally slept past noon at home after being up all night.

Claws tipped out again.

What had his jaguar *still* worked up?

Had to be Evalle not within reach.

But Storm sensed no threat in the villa. No reason to think they were about to lose her. Closing his eyes, he calmed his breathing to pull his jaguar back under control.

Something felt off.

Had his animal picked up on it? Or had the dream just been a result of indigestion from dinner in Atlanta right before the cemetery attack?

He sat up and stretched. No point in getting dressed. That dark feeling from the dream pushed at him. He headed to the bathroom to see for himself that Evalle was safe.

Stepping through the open doorway, the tightness in his chest eased just being this close to her. He waited as she emerged from the shower in a thick cloud of hot steam.

Grinning, he teased, "I think you missed a spot. But I'll find it."

She startled and tried to cover her body with her arms.

The steam cleared at the same moment.

Black veins covered half her body, maybe more.

He shouted, "What the fuck?"

"I know," she said quietly as she reached for a towel and wrapped it around her. Plenty of inky designs still tracked down her arms and legs and above her breasts. She cleared her throat. "It's okay."

"No, that is *not* okay," he argued. "That's ... " He cut himself off. Yelling about the damned lines would help no one.

Shoving his hands in his hair, he leaned back against the vanity counter. His heart raced on the edge of panic, but he had to sound reasonable or this would blow up in his face. "That's out of control, sweetheart. We have to do something. Now."

She moved to the side and started brushing her hair. "No."

"No?" He straightened, turning to her.

Slamming the brush down, she repeated, "No, as in *no* we are not bonding."

Did she think he'd just ignore those fucking lines at this point? "You gave me your word."

"If I was dying. I'm not."

His lie detector shot off the scales. Not even she believed what she said.

Now he got why his jaguar pounded at him to do something. The animal would have been breaking out on his own if he had a tangible threat to fight, but this belonged to Storm in human form. Screams echoed in his mind again.

That image of Evalle being yanked away from him flashed behind his eyes.

She'd agreed he could bond them without her consent if her issues got worse, but he would only do that if she was on death's door. Not wait until it opened, and she fell inside.

He struggled to keep his voice calm and try again. "You said we could bond immediately if your body had a significant physical change. *That* looks significant."

Crossing her arms, she breathed in and out through clenched teeth. "We agreed if I was in dire straits. I'm not."

"Lie." He called it out loud this time. He couldn't tiptoe around with her life on the line.

She stepped back as if slapped.

That gutted him.

"*Fuck!*" Storm hated this. Hated himself for not handling it better, but what if those lines were killing her? Lifting his gaze to hers, he hit her with a question he needed answered. "What aren't you telling me?"

"There's nothing to tell. I have a bunch of lines on my skin. Might be nothing more than a reaction to leaving that realm."

A lie.

Another fucking lie.

He crossed the room and back, pacing like a caged animal. She would never do that to him maliciously, but it didn't change how much hearing it cut him in half.

Stopping behind her, he waited for her to look at him in the mirror. Beautiful stubborn mate knew something. He had to get to the bottom and find out what she'd discovered.

When her wary gaze lifted, he asked, "Just tell me this. Have you learned anything about them that I don't know?"

Even without his ability to detect a lie, he saw the leading edge of her shuffle to avoid the truth as her eyes flicked away. "How would I? I've been here with you."

She also understood how to sidestep a question and reveal nothing.

"Evalle, please," he begged. "Just tell me the truth. Have you talked to someone?"

"Any answer I give doesn't matter when you've already decided everything I say is a lie."

She walked out of the bathroom.

His senses were pinging hard on her hiding something big.

Striding out behind her, he stepped into the bedroom where she dug through her suitcase with jerky motions.

Pushing her now was the hardest thing he'd ever done, but if what she held inside wouldn't harm her she would have admitted it by now. He couldn't lose her. "I thought ... we were a team to fight our battles together." His voice broke.

She flinched and froze over the chaotic pile of clothes. Dark hair fanned past her face in a curtain. Her trembling fingers clenched a pair of jeans.

Her smooth skin had turned into a canvas of ink.

Flinging the jeans back on the pile, she straightened up and turned an angry gaze on him. "The only battle going on here is *this* argument!"

"We *shouldn't* be arguing. We discussed this." He walked toward her. Anger shook his core. Not at her, never at her, but at the damage those bastards in Abandinu's realm had inflicted on his mate to bring them to this point.

Evalle hated fear. The emotion turned into rage when she couldn't manage it.

He had an intelligent mate. She had to know they had no other choice but to join his power with hers.

How much did she still possess?

Those bright green eyes of hers always gave her away. Her friends joked she could never play poker.

Her gaze darted everywhere but at him. "I'm not ready to bond."

He took the last step, leaving them inches apart. "Why won't you tell me what you know?"

That question tossed her out of step. She looked down and started digging through her clothes again. "I don't know what you're talking about."

He grabbed her wrist in a gentle grip to pull her back to him so he could figure out what the hell to do.

She yanked her arm.

Still caught.

He wouldn't let go. Ever.

Fiery green blazed in her wild gaze. She shouted, "I can't do a damn thing about this!"

"*We* can," he countered.

"No."

"*We. Can.*" His body shook with the need to protect her, to hold her close, to prove he wouldn't let her take any part of this journey alone.

His jaguar roared to save their mate.

To find the enemy and kill it.

"Don't do this, Storm." She sounded angry and shed tears, but her fear was palpable.

He held her gaze, searching for answers she wouldn't give voice to and dying inside because he had no enemy to tear apart.

The dam of terror broke inside him. He slid his hand up, curled his fingers around her wrist and pulled her hand to his lips, kissing her trembling fingers.

When he looked at her again, her face no longer tried to sell her anger. It embraced the fear she couldn't hide.

A line climbed up her neck as if taunting him.

His words were raw. "Another one just moved up your neck, sweetheart."

She lifted her hand to where he'd just glanced, stopped short, and brought her clenched fingers back down. She spoke on a choked breath. "I know. I can't stop it. If I touch a line, it spreads faster."

Truth, finally.

He held her fingers to his lips, struggling for a breath. "Please, don't leave me in the dark."

A fat tear rolled down her cheek.

He waited through a painful silence.

Finally Evalle whispered, "I talked to Adrianna." She stared at him, lost for words.

What had the witch said? He wouldn't push.

Evalle bit her bottom lip. The struggle to tell him what she knew drove his fear deeper, but she managed to get it out. "Adrianna found out ... the lines like I have killed two demons. I can't ... bond with you. I *won't*."

His heart clenched with dread for her. "What about you?"

There went her eyes again, shifting away from the truth. "She found nothing about lines on someone like me."

He heard truth in her words, but only to disguise whatever she didn't want to say.

Evalle remained stiff as a board, clearly afraid to do the wrong thing. To say the wrong thing. To make a mistake with him.

How could they have come so far to be at this point?

If only he could kill the bastards in that realm again.

He gave her arm a little tug.

That's all it took for her to come to him willingly.

He wrapped her against his body, holding her as close as his arms could tenderly. Her heart thudded just as fast as his.

But for how long would hers beat?

She hugged him the way a person clutched a life ring in the middle of the ocean with sharks circling.

He would be hers, but he wanted a chance to kill the sharks. He rocked gently from side to side, soothing her until the trembling slowed along with her choppy breaths.

Kissing the top of her head, he inhaled her scent.

He held everything he'd ever wanted in his arms right now.

No one, not even a thousand damn lines, would take her from him.

Time lost all relevance as he comforted his mate.

When she lifted her face to him, he kissed the mouth that only withheld the truth from him out of a protective streak.

Loyal mate. Incredible female. His woman.

"Don't fear me, sweetheart."

She gave him a sad nod. "I'm sorry I got mad."

Brushing hair off her face, he said, "Me, too. We'll figure this out."

She stared into his eyes and swallowed hard then closed hers. Her fingers tightened where she gripped his back. She jerked another nod, accepting his apology.

The breath that had caught in his lungs came out fast with relief. She'd let him back in.

He tried to say he'd let the bonding go, but that was too much to ask of him, or his jaguar, if Evalle ran out of all other options.

They both needed time to step back and regroup. He stroked her hair. "Are you up for a drive?"

She managed a shallow smile in return. "Sure."

It strained him to release her, but she needed the time while he showered and dressed to pull her thoughts together.

She chose a long-sleeved shirt and pants to wear.

He sensed she wanted to hide the lines from him more than the public.

After cloaking Evalle to reach their rental vehicle, Storm drove with his mate for hours. He kept the conversation easy when he wanted to pack her up and find a cure.

The sun fell out of sight, dropping a gentle blanket of dark over the desert.

That allowed her to leave the Yukon without requiring cloaking when they stopped at a true southwestern restaurant. They'd eaten and listened to music under a star-filled night sky. For that moment, she'd smiled as if she had no worries.

She did. He could feel them.

Storm made a decision right there.

Bidziil had until tomorrow morning, then he and Evalle were leaving. He'd take her back to Garwyli and see what the druid could do.

But he had a gully of doubt in his chest of her chances if they didn't bond.

As he drove past the casino to their villa, still struggling for an answer, Evalle reached over the console and caught his hand in hers. "Storm?"

She had to know. He gave her part of the truth. "I'd like to return to Treoir and see if that's better for you."

"The lines started showing up there."

She had a point.

In a light voice that sounded created just for him, she said, "Hey, maybe the seer will have something to tell me."

She kept avoiding the only option he had to offer.

He understood her fears.

If he died from the bond, that would devastate her.

That possibility was reason enough to show some patience

since the lines didn't seem to be giving her any pain or sickness.

He'd back off until tomorrow morning.

"Where does the seer live?" Evalle asked as if trying to renew his interest.

"I don't know. After listening to everyone last night, I learned that Bidziil convinced Nascha, the medicine man you met, to move closer and live in a mobile home the elders arranged for him. Bidziil said he wished their seer would do the same instead of being so stubborn because she lived farther out. Way off the beaten path, so to speak." He parked and walked around to Evalle's side.

His independent mate hadn't wanted him to open her door when they first met.

Now the simple gesture made her happy. When he opened it, she was twisted away from him in search of something. "What are you looking for?"

"Your phone's buzzing." She lifted it into view and handed the phone to him as she stepped out.

He hit the button for the speaker, answering, "Storm."

Bidziil said, "Where are you?"

"Just pulled in at the villas. What's up?"

"There's been another death. You mentioned last night that you wished you could have scented the crime scene, as we're calling it. I have guards on site making sure no one goes near."

"Excellent. When I hang up, text me the address and I'll head there."

"Will do."

Storm stuck the phone in his back pocket.

Evalle let him know she was ready. "How long will it take us to get there?"

Shit. Storm had originally wanted to have Evalle involved, but that was before he broke the dark spell on Sonny's body to release the man's spirit. Essence of the spell had tried to latch onto Storm's majik, but he blasted it to pieces by burning the spell from inside out.

He had kept that from his uncle only because it hadn't taken long to realize that neither Bidziil nor his security had any experience with majik.

The less anyone knew, the less chance the one using black

majik would know about Storm or his power. In his world, a preternatural lived or died based on knowledge of an opponent.

Storm had beaten the spell on that first corpse, but one success didn't equate being stronger than the person casting it.

If Evalle still possessed her Belador powers for fighting and gryphon energy for healing herself, he'd take her with him.

But he didn't want her around majik that had attacked him.

Definitely not when it might engage with those damned lines on her body.

Her expression changed from open and ready to grim, anticipating his reply.

He admitted, "I'd rather you didn't go with me to see this body."

"Why? I didn't throw up at the last one," she joked with an edge to her words.

"I have no doubt of your ability."

She muttered to herself and reached to push the door shut.

Storm placed his hand over hers, holding her in place.

Behind the sunglasses, her eyes narrowed. Suspicion bounced everywhere between them.

Hell, this would not go well. "I'm concerned about the majik being used on these corpses. When I broke the spell on Sonny, the residual majik looked for something to attack."

"You." She hadn't asked, just confirmed.

"Yes."

"You didn't tell me."

"No." He hated the flat line of her lips. "I didn't know what exactly the spell was, and I still don't, but my power was stronger. That's why I came out unscathed."

She pulled her hand away to cross her arms. "But I'm vulnerable."

If he said no, his gut would twist in reaction to the lie. This topic wouldn't get any better until they hashed it out. "I'm being honest with you, sweetheart. You asked for that."

"I know." She didn't sound happy about the admission.

What could he do for her?

Something inside her had broken when she was captured. Not just her body, but her heart.

It ate at him that he had nothing more to offer than the bond she fought against when she'd wanted it so much at one time.

At the moment, she stabbed him with her tense gaze, waiting

for words he didn't have to make this better.

Sounding defeated, she said, "Fine. I understand what you're saying about the dark majik."

While he loved Evalle with every inch of his heart, he hated that polite tone. "Thank you for understanding."

She barely nodded in answer and her shoulders sagged.

That slashed his heart into a hundred pieces.

Wait a minute. He had a peace offering.

"One more thing, sweetheart." When she turned to him, he said, "I will absolutely set up an invitation to the seer before I leave Bidziil tonight."

A lighter emotion trickled out from her.

As always, it took so little to make Evalle happy.

Two words came out filled with relief. "Thank you."

His heart leaped at the tinge of hope he heard. "The minute I get it all lined up, you'll be the first to know." He boosted his smile to reassure her that visiting the seer wasn't going to be a problem, or she'd back out to keep from imposing on anyone.

He didn't care who he imposed upon.

His uncle said he appreciated Storm's help.

It was time to call in a favor.

CHAPTER 14

S TORM ARRIVED AT THE VICTIM'S home close to midnight and met Bidziil outside an adobe structure much smaller and older than the villas.

His uncle led him through a home that smelled of death, but not the normal deceased-human scent Storm had encountered before. A taint of smoke and sulfur coated it, the same smells that had been on Sonny's body.

That confirmed the dark majik involved fire.

In the bedroom, the body of a young man wearing only loose shorts sat on a bed. Black hair pulled back at his neck seemed oddly undisturbed when a violent death should have resulted in a more disheveled appearance. His skin had turned to the grayish-brown shade of the dead, but still in stark contrast to the white sheets beneath him.

His chest had been cut open from neck to navel with a butcher knife that had then been shoved down at that point.

His hands still clutched the handle with a fierce grip.

Storm had never seen someone so disturbingly still while appearing fixed in the throes of an agonizing death. The twenty-something man had the wide forehead, flat nose, and high cheeks one would expect of a Native son, but his eyes bulged almost out of the sockets with pain. His facial muscles remained stretched taut from his mouth opened in a silent scream of agony.

Just like Sonny's corpse.

Both had been aware of what they were doing.

Storm cut his eyes to Bidzzil.

Sweat rolled down each side of his uncle's head and his suit hung on his haggard body. Bidziil covered his mouth with a handkerchief Storm doubted would prevent him from barfing.

After a difficult breath, Bidziil said, "His name is Imala. *Was.*

His girlfriend, Sayen, found him. We had to sedate her."

"You didn't get a chance to question her?"

"No."

Poor Bidziil might start bawling soon. Storm had to shut down his empathic senses to keep from being overloaded with his uncle's grief.

Wiping the perspiration from his pale forehead, Bidziil pulled himself together, covered his nose and spoke with a stuffy sound. "Imala's girlfriend snapped. She screamed nonstop. If her friend hadn't just dropped her off and heard the first reaction before driving away, Sayen would probably still be wailing where she found her in the hall."

Storm couldn't fault anyone for taking the woman away from the pain. She'd have to deal with enough once she regained consciousness. "Tell me what else you know about Imala."

"This sickens me. He was another bright star I've watched over since he turned twenty. He had a sharp mind and amazing people skills. I talked to him about getting into hospitality management so he could return to make a place for himself and support the clan."

Storm began to see his uncle's side of the disagreement with his father. That might be why his father had told Storm not to carry another man's burden by choice any time Storm had criticized the uncle he'd never met.

Shaking that off, Storm asked, "I scent maybe six people who have been here besides you. Two I recognize from the casino."

"Who?"

"One is Tom, the security guy you brought to the meeting last night."

Bidziil said, "He and Imala were on a baseball team."

"The other is that woman Adsila who brought our vehicle keys the first night."

Again, Bidziil nodded. "She's friends with his girlfriend and transports anyone to and from work when it's needed. I have three who do that, which could account for other scents."

Dead end there for the moment. Storm asked, "Did your people get any intel at all?"

"Yes, my man questioned Sayen's friend who drove her home from work sometimes. She said Imala would normally be at the door waiting for Sayen before he went to work at night in the casino restaurant. She also said Sayen talked all the time about the two of them and would have said something if they were having a problem. Her friend wouldn't look at the body when she dragged Sayen away. Said she feared nightmares as it was. I told her Imala had taken his life. I can't keep this quiet for long, not once Sayen is conscious again."

"Nothing makes sense in any of this, but with two deaths we finally have a common denominator." Storm waited for that to get through to his uncle.

Still looking wrung out, Bidziil's voice perked up. "Really? What is it?"

"Both were connected to your casino in some way."

His uncle deflated. "I thought about that, but most of the people in this area work there or have a family member who does."

"I know," Storm agreed. "But we have two bodies, so now we find another connection by going over everything we can until two threads cross. These two must have had more in common than casino employment."

That seemed to energize Bidziil. "Let me make arrangements for Imala's body and we'll go to my office. I'll call in everyone who can offer any information, even the elders. Maybe our covert security team will put together the dots. If we don't solve this soon, the media will destroy this place."

Storm frowned. He'd just been willing to give his uncle credit for his work to improve the tribe. Was Bidzill now concerned about a media circus that would disrupt the clan or about the casino's monetary loss by negative press?

Bidziil glanced at Storm and expelled a sigh. "Don't misunderstand me. I don't care about the loss of money, but I've watched everyone here go from destitution to building real lives. The media will destroy our community. All that being said, I don't want to lose another of my people."

Storm told himself to stop being so quick to judge when he'd always been fair with others. "Please ask everyone to step outside for a moment, Bidziil."

"You going to use your majik on it?"

"If this is the same type of spell, I have to release Imala's spirit."

Nodding with a tired movement, Bidziil stepped away. "I'll

clear the house."

Storm opened up his empathic gift just a little. He picked up genuine mourning from his uncle so heavy that sensing the emotion hurt. He'd clearly cared deeply for those two young men. He wouldn't shield anyone from this investigation.

Once the house had emptied, Storm performed the same ritual over this body.

Prepared for an attack this time, Storm squashed the rogue majik with minimum burning inside the body and managed to not light the bed on fire.

As the spirit passed over, it whispered, *Evil blossom.*

Could that be used in the spell the way sage and other herbs were to heal?

Storm headed for the door with what might just break this case tonight.

CHAPTER 15

TIRED OF GOING OVER THE same information again,
Storm said, "We're missing something. I may have to reevaluate dismissing Nascha and the seer. This has to be someone with
knowledge of how the supernatural works."

Bidziil sounded wary when he rushed to note, "Your father
had been training Nascha before he left. I trust Sani's choice of
Nascha over my own opinion."

So would Storm, but his father would be telling him to keep his
eyes open. All those years can change a person.

Rubbing his tired eyes, Storm stood his ground in the executive
suite where he, Bidziil, three elders, and three security officers
met. "I'm not accusing either person of a crime, but they might
know who is at fault. It's time to bring them in to be questioned.
What about the seer? Nascha criticized her."

"While Haloke does not have Nascha's power, her heart is in the
right place. She's been a good friend of the clan her whole life.
Many go to her for counseling as a friend as much as her ability
to find a problem."

That didn't sound as if the woman would be any help to Evalle
after all.

"Do you trust her?"

Lifting his shoulders, Bidziil said, "We have no reason not
to. Haloke stayed with us even after her son died. That speaks
volumes for her dedication to the clan."

Two elders nodded in sync with Bidziil's words.

The third old guy, Gad, had yet to warm up to Storm, but in
truth he'd been surprised the others even allowed Bidziil to invite
him.

Nothing would get solved if anyone held back information.

Sensing distrust from this elder, Storm offered, "Please speak your mind, Gad. I won't take insult."

Gad stood. "You come here and question those who have served our tribe for many years when your own father walked away."

"Gad!" Bidziil's face erupted in irritation.

There it was, the underlying anger permeating the room. Storm said, "I can't argue that point, but my father shared much about all of you and loved this tribe."

Ignoring Bidziil, Gad harrumphed. "Words mean nothing. Actions are everything."

The officers seated and standing remained silent, but their expressions denoted a keen interest in the conversation.

"Again, I agree, but my father felt for him to remain would have divided the tribe." Storm took in Bidziil's face, which registered surprise. "It's true, Bidziil. As I grew up, he told me he had been disheartened when he left. He felt all of you failed your people by not holding tight to the old ways."

Rage churned the air now, but Storm had the floor and had more to say. He might as well get it all off his chest, every bit of the truth. It would likely be his last chance to speak.

"Over the years as my father worked with the Ashaninka tribe to show them ways to improve their lives while holding on to their culture, he realized he still had to introduce new thinking so they would survive. They remained primitive in many ways, but the time he spent becoming integrated into that tribe opened his eyes to how close-minded he'd been toward Bidziil's vision for their people. My father admitted that had he been more open to new ideas, he could have been here to maintain the culture of his people during those changes just as he had for the Ashaninka. In other words, he regretted his action and the hurt he caused."

Now that Storm had spent some time with his uncle, he, too, regretted harboring anger at a man he'd never known.

Lessons learned all around.

Calm settled over the room.

The elder called Tahoma sat back. His fingers tapped on the arm of his chair. "You say 'your' people. Do you not feel any tie to this tribe?"

Bidziil jumped in. "Why should he? From the moment he showed up, Storm has been treated as an outsider. I was angry when Sani left, but I've also seen our culture slowly disintegrate.

That's why I formed a committee to do as Sani had wanted to maintain the old ways." He glared at the elders. "You three argued with me."

Gad grumbled something under his breath. "You wanted to bring in outsiders."

"Most of them were *Dine!*" Bidziil argued. He evidently needed to get a few things off his chest, too. Grief would do that. He wasn't done. "We have to do more to save our past and protect our future. Look around the Dine nation. Every clan is doing this in some way."

The last elder spoke, which surprised Storm, because Yazzle appeared so timid he leaned with the strongest wind. "I will do a better job supporting the committee, Bidziil."

The other two gave Yazzle a glare that accused him of being the class suck-up.

On a roll, Bidziil said, "Thank you, Yazzle, but all of you fought me on sending our people to college."

Tahoma said, "Wait a minute, Bidziil. I supported that with my own funds."

"Yes, you did, until you realized they were accepting placements outside the reservation."

Shrugging, Tahoma said, "I don't like money leaving our land. You shouldn't have left either."

Bidziil appeared ready to yank his hair out. "Had I not gone to a university with specific studies, I might not have understood the fine print attached to our sovereignty. No one could build a house or start a business on land they owned, but we have worked around that, haven't we?"

Grumbling acknowledgement circled the room.

Storm continued to reevaluate the negative attitude he'd arrived with, which was good for the soul.

But this group strayed from the reason for the meeting.

He wanted to find the dark majik user.

This bunch could hold board meetings on their own time.

Before he had a chance to return them to the discussion, Gad said, "I'm surprised you don't know more about this clan."

Taken aback, Storm asked, "Why would you think that when my father and I lived thousands of miles away in a remote jungle location?"

"Haloke claimed she kept up with Sani through dream walking."

Hairs along Storm's neck stood.

He searched his mind frantically for any mention of Haloke, but his father spoke only of the tribe as a whole with the exception of a few specific people. Storm assumed other memories held too much pain.

Storm knew in that second he'd missed something significant and this could be it. "My father *never* spoke of a person called Haloke. How did she know him?" Storm sent that last question in Bidziil's direction.

Tahoma turned another look of surprise on Storm and spoke before Bidziil could. "Your father *never* mentioned *her*? They were very close growing up. Many thought those two would become a powerful couple."

Bidziil said, "Sani would not have called her Haloke. She only took that name when she mourned his leaving and felt she had lost that part of her."

"That's right," Tahoma agreed.

Concern crawled up Storm's spine. His hands dampened. "What would he have known her by?"

"Miakoda."

Blood rushed hard through Storm, pounding his ears. "My father mentioned Miakoda one time many years ago. I can't recall much beyond him saying he was sad over leaving her as she was. I didn't understand what he meant without further information, but I never pressed him for more than he wanted to share."

Bidziil said, "When your father made up his mind to leave, he went to tell her. Afterwards, he came to see me and said she had a broken heart he couldn't heal."

The door opened and Nascha entered, anger burning in his gaze. "I have come to this den of traitors, as you demanded." The grim old guy crossed his arms.

Bidziil sighed loud enough to be heard down the hall. "This is not a den of traitors and I sent a request, not a demand."

Lifting a wrinkled hand, Nascha said, "I did not come to argue. State what you need so I may leave."

"Storm would like to talk to you."

Expecting the crotchety old guy to refuse, Storm addressed Nascha first with respect. "I consider any time you allow me an honor, old one. My father spoke of you as his friend."

At that, Nascha's taut shoulders relaxed a tiny bit. "My friend should have stayed."

"My father taught me every action is for a reason as it creates a ripple effect like a stone tossed into a calm lake. Without the movement, life remains stagnant. While you may not forgive him for leaving, he told me he felt you would never reach your full potential had he stayed. He believed you would have been a great support to him, but his people needed a powerful medicine man. He saw a better future for his people in what you would offer as their medicine man, not him."

Bidziil listened with rapt attention.

Storm had spoken the truth. Now he waited to see what the medicine man's power might feel like if Nascha dropped his guard or lost control.

Nascha bowed his head then lifted it up. "Your father honored me with his belief. He told me often that I should take this position, but he spoke the truth. I would never have stepped in had he stayed. I have given all I can to my people since he left and feel I have grown into my power, but I still miss him."

A lump formed in Storm's throat. "As do I."

"Is that all you have to ask Nascha, Storm?" Yazzle said, breaking the solemn moment.

Bidzzil snapped, "Do not rush this talk."

Yazzle whined, "Nascha sounds like he wants to get out of here."

Nascha cast a glance filled with dark humor at Yazzle. "You would be wise to remain in your role of tribal mouse with giant head."

For all his timidity, Yazzle sent the old guy an angry look.

Storm drew everyone's attention back to the problem at hand. "I need your expertise to find the person responsible for killing tribal members." When Nascha lifted his chin in acknowledgment, Storm explained what had happened to Imala, which had parallels with Sonny's death. When he finished, he realized the elders hadn't known all the details, such as Storm freeing the spirits and the dark majik attacking him.

Too bad.

He had no time to dance around this topic when he could feel they were close to figuring it out. "You said dark spirits walk among us. What were you referencing, Nascha?"

"I saw one in the morgue and another near the casino."

"What?" Bidziil snapped. "And you didn't tell me?"

Speaking in a deep voice roughened by many years of chanting and singing, Nascha said, "Storm just repeated what I said. You have been told twice!" Drawing a breath, Nascha stepped back with a sudden realization. "You brought me here to accuse me of performing these acts? I do *not* touch evil majik."

Clearly the peacemaker, Bidziil said, "No, of course not."

Yazzle's eyes bulged. "Not me."

Gad shoved a dismissive hand in Nascha's direction. "No."

Tahoma's eyebrows furrowed, as he remained silent.

Nascha snarled at Tahoma. "I am not like you. I do not wish for power."

Opening his hands from where he'd had his arms folded, Tahoma said, "I'm not accusing, but you are the most powerful in this area. If you aren't doing this, you should know who is."

Storm confirmed, "Nascha is not the one responsible."

"How can you know?" Tahoma challenged.

"First of all, I would know if he lied. Second, he doesn't carry dark energy."

Gad sat forward. "How would you know *either* of those things?"

Lifting an eyebrow in Bidziil's direction, Storm waited for permission to explain.

Bidziil said in a forlorn voice, "Might as well tell them, Storm."

"I am half-Ashaninka, as many of you know by now. What you don't know is I am also a Skinwalker."

Tension and fear burst through the room.

Even the security guards leaned back.

Sending a look Nascha's way, Storm found him standing still and not running from the battle.

Continuing, Storm said, "I received some gifts and some liabilities with that side of my blood. I am a strong empathic and can detect a lie." He wouldn't share how lying on his part resulted in a painful backlash.

Yazzle snapped his fingers. "We can line up everyone to face Storm. If they lie about being the killer, he'll know."

Nascha made a scoffing sound. "You think someone who

possesses that much power will be so easily caught? Fool."

When Nascha spoke of that much power, Storm asked, "Who in the tribe, besides you, wields power, Nascha?"

Bidziil interjected, "No one other than Haloke, but even Nascha criticizes her power."

Nascha muttered, "Why do you defend Bird Woman?"

Appearing beat down and out of patience, Bidziil struggled to sound respectful. "Did you not just complain to us at the morgue about Haloke lacking in skill?"

"Yes. I tell you her sight is not clear."

"Same thing, right?" Bidziil snapped with exasperation. "We are bringing her in, too. She'd be here now, but out of respect I asked you first to avoid you two being together."

Storm pulled at all the threads dangling in this case. "Do you think Haloke is powerful, Nascha?"

"Last time I saw her, she had *little* power."

"See?" Bidziil complained. "Riddles."

"When was that?" Storm asked.

"Two years back when her son died. I tried to help her heal. She turned away from me. She was not same person."

Bidziil said, "I've already told Storm about Sani breaking her heart and she hasn't been the same."

"Not broken heart. She has broken soul," Nascha said, anger picking up in his voice. "I keep trying to tell you she does not see clear."

Storm lifted a hand, asking Bidziil not to argue, then presented a new question to Nashca. "Do you think she could be performing dark majik?"

Grasping his jaw, Nascha stared unfocused for seconds. "I have found no evidence of it on those she sent to me."

"We're back to square one," Yazzle complained.

Feeling as if he was on to something, Storm asked, "Who taught Haloke to be a seer?"

Lowering his hand, Nascha said, "Sani."

CHAPTER 16

E VALLE FINISHED HER KICKBOXING MOVEMENTS, a
skill she sometimes needed, which came in handy when she
wore her boots with hidden blades to patrol Atlanta. Standard
gear to walk the streets on the lookout for demons or other threats
to humans.

Would she ever need them again?

"No negative waves," she ordered the empty great room in the
villa, but the phrase made her smile. It came from that old *Kelly's
Heroes* movie, one of Feenix's favorites.

Was her little gargoyle still having fun in Treoir?

Did he miss her?

She knew he did and that Daegan could zap them back there.
Feenix just seemed so far away.

With her workout complete, she showered, cursed the lines
continuing to fill up her skin, then tackled the remote for the
television. That said everything about her level of boredom.

Tossing it aside, she went on the patio and lounged for as long
as she could sit still.

No eagle flew around, much less stopped by to visit when she
could use a sympathetic ear.

The first time must have been a dream.

Well, damn. She'd felt special by that bird showing up.

As the night wore on with no word from Storm, she debated on
calling Adrianna until she realized the time.

After four in the morning here.

She did the time zone math. Still too early to call Adrianna
when she had no news.

Besides, she had to get her head straightened out.

No more giving Storm a hard time when all he wanted to do
was protect her from doing something dangerous.

He'd told her the truth in the car, just as she'd asked.

And he'd been right.

Could she fight off a dark majik spell? Doubtful.

The kickboxing had helped. With sunrise still a ways off, she could go for a brisk walk around the resort in the dark.

That would burn off her nervous energy.

Her heart wanted to jump out of her chest after that last look in the mirror. The lines were expanding faster.

She ran to the bedroom and stepped into a black one-piece outfit with long legs she liked to wear for sword practice.

Tying the halter around her neck on her way to the bathroom, she paused to brush her hair into a ponytail.

Two patches of line crept around her forearm as she watched.

"Think I care, Universe?" she snarled. Fuck. What had she done to deserve this?

The room didn't answer.

She missed Feenix. He might not have many words in his vocabulary, but he'd at least say something.

She put her sneakers on and descended the stairs.

When she reached the door, she cursed. Her glasses were upstairs, and she couldn't go out with glowing green eyes around humans. As she turned to retrieve her glasses, she caught a look in the mirror in the foyer.

A weave of black lines ran from her scalp onto her cheek below her left eye.

Her not-bright-green eye.

Both eyes were ... dark.

They no longer glowed.

Her stomach hit her feet.

The doorbell chimed.

She couldn't move. Her Alterant beast and the gryphon she'd evolved into had been responsible for her glowing gaze. This couldn't be. She wanted to scream at losing all she'd been.

The doorbell chimed again.

She couldn't move.

That damn doorbell wouldn't stop.

She started to kick the door, but she'd probably break her damned foot. In no mood to see anyone, she peered through the peephole.

Adsila.

If Evalle didn't answer, the woman would probably report she wasn't home, and Storm might rush back thinking she had a problem. He couldn't see her like this.

He'd launch into the bonding. She'd agreed. This would qualify as dire straits.

Screw it. Maybe her face would send the woman running. Evalle opened the door and did her best to sound civil. "Yes?"

No shock registered in Adsila's expression. She probably met all kinds of strange people at a casino and thought she addressed a human with a fetish for crazy ink.

Hell, Evalle might be a human at this point.

"We didn't officially meet last night. I'm Adsila. I'm sorry to disturb you at this hour."

Digging deep to show some manners, Evalle acted as if her face didn't sport a gang tattoo. "You're not disturbing me. What can I do for you?"

Pasting her hospitality smile in place, Adsila said, "I'm here to take you to the seer. She'd like to meet you."

"What? Really?" Evalle's heart raced. Would the seer even speak to her once she saw these lines? Her hands shook. She clasped them to stop the trembling and asked, "Did Storm set this up ... or Bidziil?"

Adsila nodded, another polite motion. "Yes. They're in a big meeting with security. I was told to come right away, that this is important to you."

As if that wasn't obvious in the switch from bitch Evalle to happy Evalle?

Best mate ever. She wanted to have Storm say the same about her. Maybe the seer could give her some answers.

Evalle had been ready to give up all hope a moment ago.

This couldn't have come at a better time. She gave herself tiny kudos for opening the door in spite of her screwed-up looking face.

"I'm in a little bit of a hurry if you're ready," Adsila said, though still in a patient tone.

"Now? Sure. I have to be back by daylight."

"I see no problem in that, but it's a little bit of a drive so we should get moving."

"Sorry, yes." Evalle looked around in a rush then at herself. She didn't carry a purse and had a code to the door. Done. "I'm ready." She stepped out, locked up then fell into pace with Adsila's fast steps leading to a Suburban still running.

Storm had been doing his best not to hover.

Evalle appreciated how he hadn't asked her to wait so he could go with her.

Good mate. He showed his trust and made her feel strong.

CHAPTER 17

S TORM RAN AN AGITATED HAND over his hair.

Nascha claimed Storm's father had trained Haloke.

Keeping his voice respectful, Storm told Nascha, "But Sani has been gone many years and I can assure you he never practiced dark majik."

"That is true," Nascha stated. "That is why she is not best seer. She never sought more knowledge."

Bidziil stood. "That's wrong."

Nascha growled, "Why? Why do you defend her?"

Sounding ready to bite nails in half, Bidziil said, "I'm only filling in information. Two years back, after her son died, Haloke asked me for money to visit another clan to study under a seer revered among our tribe. I gave her funds because *you* kept complaining about her, Nascha. She returned ten months later saying she would be more powerful than ever."

"Based on those Haloke sent with message of how to heal their Hózhó, I saw little improvement," Nascha snarled, defiance in every word.

Everything came together in Storm's mind. "Are you positive Haloke trained under the powerful seer?"

Bidziil opened his mouth and closed it.

Nascha pointed at Bidziil. "Ha. She spend your money doing nothing."

"Or ... " Storm started, hating what he had to suggest. "She could have been training under someone *else*." Turning to Bidziil, he asked, "You said she lost her son right before she left on sabbatical. Isn't that the boy you told me ended up shot by a gang member for running drugs at college?"

"Yes. I was angry and hurt. I'd gone to great lengths to find him a suitable placement so he could come back and help his mother, maybe convince her to live closer to the clan."

Storm's heart rate picked up speed. "Has anyone died unusually before now?"

"No."

"What about any animals?" Storm pressed.

"Not really—"

"Yes, there was one," Yazzle said, shocking everyone when he spoke up. "I heard about a wild coyote found dead in grotesque ways."

"Why didn't you tell me?" Bidziil shouted.

His security team groaned and started talking among themselves.

"Now dead animals will solve this?" Tahoma asked, getting annoyed all over again.

"Describe the carcass," Storm directed Yazzle.

"I didn't see it. Just heard some boys talking about finding a coyote corpse intact except for the eyes and heart. The coat had strips of fur burned off and the claws had grown double the natural length."

Bidziil asked Storm, "What are you thinking?"

"I need to talk to Haloke to determine if we're on the right track before throwing suspicion at an innocent person." Actually, he would pick up dark energy as soon as he got near her if she was the one, but he wouldn't point a finger at anyone without evidence.

He had to find Evalle first to explain that he was visiting the woman but couldn't take her. That wouldn't go over well at all. Maybe he'd just deal with the seer then go home to Evalle.

Looking to Bidziil, Storm said, "I'll let you know what I find out."

"I'll go with you," Bidziil said.

"Thank you, but I should go alone."

Nascha offered, "I should join you in this meeting."

"Thank you, old one, but I believe keeping you as far from her as possible is best for the tribe if she is using dark majik. You are of the light and none of us would want that exposed to this level of evil."

"What of you?" the medicine man challenged.

"I will be fine. She has no idea what she's risking if she attacks me with dark majik." Storm couldn't say for sure that he knew what he would face, but unless Haloke had ever gone up against demon blood, he could hold his own.

At a minimum, he should be able to protect himself from her majik.

Should being the operative word.

His last statement had shifted the way everyone looked at Storm from worry over his safety to wariness.

He couldn't help that.

Before he left, he returned to an earlier topic now that he had a potential suspect. "Back to my question about blossom. Does anyone know if Haloke has ever referenced that word in any way?"

Happy to be the one in the know, Yazzle said, "Not unless you're talking about Adsila."

"Adsila?" Storm asked with a sick feeling.

Yazzle sounded proud of himself. "That's what she told me her name means." He sighed. "She's truly a blossom."

The calm Gad leaned forward and yelled at Yazzle, "You tell us now? Storm asked if we knew a person named Blossom or if anyone used that term in referencing something."

"He didn't ask me," Yazzle complained, eyes widening as he probably just realized his infatuation with Adsila might be a mistake.

Storm grabbed his head, ready to turn his roaring jaguar loose. His animal had had enough of this bunch and so had he. They both wanted to check on Evalle after hearing Adsila might be involved.

He said, "Yazzle's right. He was in the bathroom while that came up and we were onto something else when he returned. *'Evil blossom'* is what Imala's spirit whispered to me as it left his body. Before we accuse someone of a crime, did Adsila have any contact with Sonny or Imala specifically on the days of their deaths?"

The head of security stood and had his electronic pad up, reading it. He said, "She punched out from work two hours prior to Sonny's death and ... was off duty four hours before Imala's. She should have been at work both times."

Bidziil said, "I want her brought up, but don't make a scene so she doesn't run."

"Yes, sir," his head of security replied, "Let me call down and determine if she's still on the property."

"She should be," Bidziil said. "We had a tech issue she intended to stay tonight and track down."

Nodding, the officer walked off to use his radio.

Directing his words at Bidziil, Storm said, "Tell me how to get to Haloke." As he listened, he ended his mental debate over what to do about Evalle. In the past, he'd normally tell her before going.

For any hope of getting their life back, he had to continue treating her the same way and speak to her first.

When Bidziil finished with the directions, Storm said, "I'll wait to talk to Adsila. If she's the one behind this, you won't be able to handle her. As soon as she's contained, I'll know how to approach Haloke."

The head of security walked back flanked by his two other men. He said, "Adsila is gone. She signed out a car in the name of Tso to transport someone to the seer."

"Why take it in my name?" Bidziil asked.

Fuck. Storm said, "Not you. Me." He yanked his phone out and called Evalle.

No answers.

Bidziil said, "What do you think Adsila is doing?"

Storm knew in his heart where Evalle was because he'd been played. He yanked the keys from his pocket and turned for the door. "She's taking Evalle to the seer. How long ago did she sign out her car?"

The security guy said, "Thirty-three minutes."

Storm roared.

CHAPTER 18

EVALLE HAD SECOND THOUGHTS. SHE should've waited for Storm to join her on this trip to the seer.

But that might have meant missing this opportunity.

She couldn't put this off.

He almost snapped this morning. What would he do the minute he saw her eyes no longer glowed?

Bond with her.

Enough with the mental chatter, even if it was more than she could get from Adsila who drove with a single-minded focus.

The young woman had a heavy foot on the gas pedal for an employee, but during the drive from the villa she'd spoken little. The only time she sounded the least bit interested in the conversation had been when Evalle asked what else she did at the resort.

According to Adsila, she had a serious gift for technology.

She'd said Bidziil couldn't truly appreciate her skill, because he had so little ability.

Arrogant much?

Evalle lost interest in conversing after that.

They might be traveling down the same roads Evalle and Storm had taken earlier but being out here in the night changed the feeling from tourist to interloper.

Adsila slowed the car.

Evalle looked for a turnoff. None.

That didn't stop Adsila from taking a hard right and driving through the desert.

Huh? Evalle looked around. "Uhm, where are we going?"

"To the seer. She doesn't live near the noise and chaos around electronics. It interferes with her powers."

Storm had described the seer's home as way off the beaten path.

He hadn't been exaggerating.

Evalle had never felt unease at being around humans, but she did now. Was that because she hadn't been able to tap any of her powers earlier?

Probably. This must be how a human would feel around a preternatural.

Never think like prey.

Wrong frame of mind.

Even without them, she still had fighting skills and reflexes sharper than a human's.

What brought on those thoughts?

Her gaze traveled to where she clutched her leg to keep it from bouncing with nervous energy. Black lines split and crawled two more inches down her right arm, filling in a blank area. How long before they covered her entire body and linked together?

She checked her left arm. A new outbreak squiggled around to the under side. She should have stopped to grab a watch or phone, but Adsila had been in such a hurry and Evalle had just faced the demise of her powers.

No powers and black veins that might turn deadly.

She'd been in panic mode and jumped at the chance to go.

Hopefully, the seer would have something useful to share.

How could she and Storm have a life if Evalle had no control over her body any more?

The car bounced over bumps and the tires dipped into holes. Adsila steered with skill, avoiding short fat bushes that turned the terrain into a living obstacle course.

They slowed as the headlights reached a round structure. Storm had talked about the older structures a few members still lived in today, but this one caught Evalle by surprise. "Is that a hogan?"

"Yes."

"The seer lives *there*?" Evalle couldn't hide her surprise at the dwelling for someone the tribe revered.

"Haloke holds to the old ways as any strong seer should," Adsila replied in a terse tone.

How dare this woman chastise Evalle just for questioning the hut.

Not Bidziil's best representative for the casino.

It didn't matter. Evalle would not complain after the woman had driven her to meet with the seer.

Evalle would have likely gotten lost on her own.

Adsila parked.

A fiftyish woman in a blousy pale-blue top with multiple strands of beaded necklaces appeared at the opening where light flickered from inside the hogan. Her dark skirt made of geometric designs stopped short of her ankles. Silver ran through her black hair, which fell loose to her chest. She had an attractive face Evalle could see being used on brochures about Native culture.

This must be the seer.

As Evalle got out, a large eagle swooped down and landed on an arm the woman extended.

The bird lifted its head and stared at Evalle through dark eyes that appeared as black holes. She squinted. Was her night vision going?

Or ... was it gone?

The eagle reminded her of the bird she'd dreamed about. Maybe not a dream.

Just like the one on the patio, this bird didn't so much as twitch a feather.

"Welcome, Evalle. I am Haloke," she said in a warm voice.

Smiling to hide her misgivings over seeing the eagle again, Evalle said, "Thank you for the invitation, Haloke. I'm humbled you agreed to meet me."

"It is an honor. I knew your mate's father."

That was a surprise. Maybe that was why Storm felt confident he could arrange this meeting.

Should it surprise Evalle that Haloke called Storm her *mate* when Adsila had referred to her as Storm's wife?

He probably referred to her status that way when he set this up.

"I have to go, Mother Haloke. Will Roy find peace tonight?" Adsila asked in a longing voice.

"Yes, child."

Adsila turned toward the car she'd left with the motor running again.

Evalle had to remind Adsila not to forget her. "Are you coming back in enough time to return before daylight?"

Adsila paused then angled her head with a glance at Haloke before her gaze went to Evalle. "Storm will come."

"Oh, well shoot. That's okay then." Storm would bring the vehicle he'd placed a protective coating on. He'd be here for sure before sunrise. "Thank you for the ride, Adsila," Evalle said, trying to be polite while grinding her teeth at the woman.

Adsila could have mentioned earlier Storm would be coming.

Evalle relaxed a little.

Storm knew so much more than her about medicine men, shamans, and seers. Wouldn't it be a nice surprise if Haloke figured out how to fix Evalle by the time Storm showed up?

Haloke spoke with gentle authority. "You have questions for me?"

Taking a deep breath, Evalle prepared to explain all she could without giving up the secrets she had to shield. "I don't know exactly how this works, but here's what's bothering me. I was kidnapped recently and put in a place that ... " Evalle struggled for words that would accurately convey the physical abuse and mage's spell she'd suffered in Abandinu's realm. "Let's just say a bad place and I left with some issues."

"You were tortured?"

"Yes."

"You are not one with yourself."

Finally, someone described Evalle's inner turmoil. She felt separated from who she'd been for so long. There were two people inside her—Evalle before the kidnapping and Evalle after the rescue.

Everyone kept waiting for her to be the before version. She did, too.

She'd once been a warrior, mate, friend, and gryphon shifter.

She came back a ... shell, unable to find those parts again.

With no better idea of how to put all that across, she simply asked, "Is my Hózhó broken?"

Evidently she'd surprised the seer with knowing that word. The seer smiled. "Hózhó is not a thing, but all that surrounds you and is within." The seer stroked her eagle and whispered words that sounded affectionate.

Returning to Evalle, Haloke said in a light voice, "I understand you do not wish to bond with Storm."

Why would he tell the seer that?

Maybe it was the only way he could gain Evalle an interview.

She wouldn't fault him for sharing that after all he probably went through to make this happen.

"We're still talking about bonding," Evalle said, noncommittal.

"Why do you hesitate?"

Why was Haloke asking about something personal? Evalle held her patience and admitted, "My messed up Hózhó, for one reason. I want to feel whole again before I do that."

"You will heal. You hurt Storm by not bonding."

Evalle mentally sagged with a new load of guilt. She'd see this through for him. That reminded her to ask, "Do you see the lines on my face and arms?"

"Yes. That is why I had you brought to me."

"How would you know?" Evalle mumbled more to herself.

Haloke stroked her bird and said, "My eagle brought news of your struggles."

Evalle gave the bird another look, but the bird's body and head blurred a moment then came back into focus. Her throat dried up.

She coughed and asked, "He talks?"

"She," Haloke corrected. "We need no words to communicate. She shares her memories with me."

Squinting to focus on the seer and her nonverbal bird, Evalle said, "I ... I don't understand."

Haloke started singing as she smiled at her eagle.

Light began to glow brighter inside the hogan behind the seer until she stood in an electric aura.

Evalle stared hard, trying to figure out why that happened. The longer she looked, the more she felt drawn to the light and took a step forward.

Continuing in a soothing tone, Haloke said, "Walk with me, Evalle. We will go where I can help you."

That sounded like a champion idea.

Evalle stumbled on her first step, caught her balance and joined Haloke as they walked around the hogan.

The eagle took flight into a black sky lit only by an unfinished moon.

Watching the majestic bird glide, Evalle murmured, "So beautiful."

Haloke lifted her hand, moving it slowly in front of Evalle. "You wish to fly as the eagle does. This is your heart's desire."

True, but Evalle felt so relaxed and at peace, she sighed. "Yes, I want that."

"Your mate has a cat inside and you have wings."

Haloke said the nicest things. She definitely understood.

Evalle smiled, "Yes. His jaguar is amazing."

"You are more than amazing," Haloke said. "You have giant wings."

"Yes, they're beautiful." Evalle smiled at the compliment. "I can change into a ... " She lost her train of thought. Had she almost said gryphon?

She couldn't share that, right?

Haloke said, "You must open up for this to work."

That made sense. The seer couldn't help if she held back.

Lifting a hand, Evalle rubbed her forehead. She'd never taken drugs, but she felt weird and happy at the same time.

Her feet walked on soft ground as if it had turned into a cloud. She chuckled.

That sounded stupid. Good thing she hadn't said it out loud.

"You may talk to me, Evalle," Haloke encouraged. "I will protect your secrets. They are weighing you down and keeping you from flying."

Evalle's heart thumped slow, but hard beats. She envisioned being a gryphon again and Storm thrilled at watching her fly. He wanted that, too.

She asked Haloke, "Are you sure I'll fly again?"

"Oh, yes. We must make your Hózhó whole first, then you will be complete."

Yes. To be whole, Evalle mused silently. To be the woman Storm had mated. She wanted him to be proud of her again.

She desperately wanted her gryphon back.

But she'd take having her powers and getting rid of these black lines, if nothing else.

Lifting her hands, Evalle watched with disconnected curiosity as the lines moved frenetically over her skin. She followed each movement, fascinated by the designs created.

Was this what floating in a dream felt like?

Or was she hallucinating again?

She couldn't find the energy to care.

Haloke stopped, shaking Evalle from her relaxing moment.

She looked around to a cold fire pit. "Where are we?"

"This is my sacred spot, the place I will heal you." Haloke reached into a pocket on her skirt. She spoke strange words then tossed shiny chips of what looked like glass at the pit.

A fire sparked to life.

Evalle shook her head.

Something was wrong.

Healing.

Storm said a seer did not heal. Evalle's eyes were locked on the robust flames. Haloke had started a fire the way someone like ... Adrianna would.

Adrianna?

Warning bells rang in Evalle's head, but in a slow dull gong. Evalle took a wobbly step back and lifted a hand to her head. The landscape moved around her. She mumbled, "Wait. Are you a seer or witch?"

Haloke shouted and her eagle screeched.

The bird swooped across the fire, sending a wave of smoke into Evalle's face. She inhaled a strong anise smell and choked on her next breath.

Singing reached her ears as if the sound came through a tunnel.

Haloke raised her voice and the world spun faster. She tried to move, get away.

The eagle bumped her from behind.

She stumbled to her knees in front of the fire. Bright flames danced in her gaze and wouldn't let her go. Smoke flowed over and through her.

Haloke shouted, "Mate of Storm, rise and prepare to be healed."

Evalle lost all control of her body and stood upon command. "I'm ready," she murmured. Her head argued, but Evalle couldn't understand Haloke's words.

No longer singing, the seer spoke undecipherable words in a harsh tone full of authority.

The fire burst alive with color.

Evalle's vision blurred.

Close to her ear, Haloke said, "Are you ready to surprise your mate with your new Hózhó?"

"Am I ... healed?" Evalle asked in a slurred voice.

"Not quite. You must do one more thing then you will fly with the eagle."

CHAPTER 19

STORM RAN AT TOP SPEED in his jaguar form through the dark desert. His animal's sharp night vision allowed them to leap over or sweep around any obstacle. He'd shifted outside the resort property as soon as he reached the first place he could free his jaguar without starting mass chaos.

His animal had been tearing at him the whole time.

As Storm rushed away, Bidziil had shouted that he'd catch up by car and deal with Haloke.

Not if Storm's jaguar reached the woman first.

For her sake, he'd better find Evalle unharmed.

As he streaked across a paved road, his jaguar found fresh ruts where a vehicle carrying Adsila's scent had driven.

That should make finding Haloke even quicker.

Storm's jaguar caught Evalle's scent when he reached a hogan. He slid to a stop, sending dust flying, stuck his head inside only long enough to determine the place was empty.

Inhaling the scent of his mate, his jaguar tore around the structure and stretched out his stride to eat up ground.

In seconds, he had a small fire in view.

A narrow figure stood silhouetted against the glow. Too short to be Evalle, but that's where her scent led him. His jaguar snarled and raced forward.

Thirty yards out, he slowed his animal.

Storm wouldn't hesitate to enter the territory of a deadly witch, but neither would he put Evalle in further jeopardy by blasting in with no idea what was going on.

As his animal slowed, it snarled and growled. Storm apologized to his jaguar and forced a fast shift that ripped his body in opposing directions.

He lost no time, striding to the fire where the seer stood. Who else could it be? "Where is she, Haloke?"

"Evalle is healing herself."

"Liar. Tell me now or I'll let my jaguar out and rip you apart."

"That will not provide answers," she said, full of confidence.

She had no idea what she faced.

Storm let the demon roll over him long enough for his eyes to glow red.

Losing her cocky smile, Haloke hissed, "Get away from me, demon."

"As if you aren't evil incarnate? Where the fuck is she?" He followed Evalle's scent in one direction then stopped when he scented a different path. Rushing around the fire while Haloke stood motionless as a statue, Storm picked up a third trail.

Then a fourth. Fuck! "Which way did she go? Tell me now and you'll have a head start."

"Why would I need that?" Haloke sounded too confident.

He swung around, shoving his red-eyed glare in her face. "To run from me." That came out in a demonic voice.

Her eyes flared wide, but she stood firm. "I'm helping Evalle."

"*Liar!*" Which way had his mate gone? He knew without a doubt every second counted.

She tossed something into the fire. Smoke boiled around Storm. When the smoke dispensed, he said, "Didn't work, bitch."

Her face fell and her hands shook.

"You're losing your chance to run. What did you do to Evalle?"

"Healed her," Haloke started on a shaky breath. "I saw the damage in her. No one helped my Roy."

Storm strained to prevent his jaguar from breaking out and shredding her, but he still had no idea which direction Evalle had departed here. Running in any single direction risked choosing wrong and losing precious seconds.

His heartbeat went into double time. He sucked air in and out, filtering the smells to find the strongest one left by his mate. He had to calm down enough to think when dealing with a lunatic. "We had nothing to do with Roy."

"You are blood of Bidziil," she spat back at him as if that explained everything.

Wait, it just might.

Both young men were his uncle's protégés and Bidziil had been trying to show that he cared about Storm. He'd also helped to get Haloke's kid in college.

His uncle was the connection.

"Bidziil did right by you and your son."

"*Roy was all I had!* Bidziil sent him away. My child never came back. I gave up everything for him, to give him the life he deserved. He would be here now, married to Adsila if Bidziil hadn't turned him against me. Bidziil must pay!"

Shit. Storm had nothing that would break through her insanity if she was killing to pay his uncle back for her son's death.

He couldn't wait any longer. He had to choose a direction.

Storm strode past Haloke as light grew, pushing the dark away behind him in the east. He had nothing but a gut feeling drawing him west, but he'd learned to trust his senses.

Haloke's voice powered up, calling to the wind to kill the son of Sani.

She could try.

Ten steps from the fire, wind swirled, spinning sand to slap his naked body.

That damn witch thought to stop him?

She'd just confirmed he headed in the right direction. Even the wind couldn't steal Evalle's scent from him once he got away from Haloke's majik.

He leaped forward to run.

Wind churned faster and faster, building a sand tornado that tossed him from side to side.

Storm covered his eyes, disoriented.

He tried to push forward. Sunrise was on the way. He had to find Evalle and cloak her.

His jaguar wouldn't stop until he found their mate.

Storm called up his animal. It blasted to life and dove into the wind, flipping around. Wind tossed his jaguar and battered him in the air. His animal landed hard outside the tornado.

Haloke came running up, shouting words as fast as a machine gun spitting out bullets.

Jumping up, he turned in a circle then finally saw a lone figure standing in the distance on the other side of Haloke.

He lunged forward.

A new wind shoved him back.

Storm had never put his jaguar through so many changes at one time, but he shifted again. The second he stood on two feet, Storm unleashed his own dark shit. He roared words he'd never intended to speak again.

Haloke had learned how to wield dark majik.

Storm had been born into it.

His majik lived and breathed.

His father's power came from the light. That side of Storm warned him Evalle had seconds left until something terrible happened.

With one last shouted curse, the wall of wind wobbled.

That was his chance.

He called to his demon blood and shifted again into his jaguar, hoping he hadn't harmed his animal. He could take damage better in that form with the dark blood coursing through him.

Haloke gasped, eyes wide in terror.

She screamed for the gods to kill the demon!

Yeah, bad move pissing off a Skinwalker, bitch.

Storm's jaguar roared and dove through the wall of wind-whipped sand, closing his eyes at the last moment. Sharp stones in the whirling vortex ripped at his coat. Blood spun free in long strands. His jaguar forced one paw ahead of the next, walking through a living buzz saw.

CHAPTER 20

E VALLE FINISHED REMOVING HER CLOTHES.
Haloke's chant played in the gentle wind. The seer had said
Evalle had to first shed her garments to be free of all restraint,
which made sense before she met her gryphon again.

Shifting naked made the transition easier.

Next, she had to peel her inner being to the core, to find the true
Evalle. Doing that reminded her what Adrianna called meditation.

Evalle had never been so at peace.

Her mind grasped a thought and let it go just as easily.

The world stretched far below her in a beautiful canyon, begging
her to join the eagle. Air swirled around her in a hazy gray light
getting brighter every few seconds.

Who are you, Evalle? Haloke's voice asked all around her.

"I am me. I am Belador. I am Storm's mate."

Words swirled, flowing in and out of her head in Haloke's voice.
The seer had said she wouldn't leave Evalle, that she'd be with her
to the end.

What end?

Evalle waited for an answer, but Haloke's voice filled her head
again. *You must not interrupt the healing, Evalle. This will only
work once. You want to fly, right?*

"Yes, I want to fly. I want to bond. I want to shift into my
gryphon ... " Evalle murmured, repeating the things Haloke had
chanted with her until the desire took on a life.

A river of calm moved steadily through her chest, splitting off
and pooling in her arms and legs. Warm air caressed her skin.
Loose hair teased her face.

Evalle peered over the edge of the cliff into what Haloke had
called the Grand Canyon and awaited her destiny.

Light continued to soften the darkness, just enough for her

vision to make out the wide gulf of air between her and the cliffs she faced across the canyon. Still blurry, but that would clear up. The seer had said so.

A warning niggled at her.

Why? She closed her eyes with nothing to fear standing here with her body and soul free of the world.

No more fear.

That felt so good.

Haloke said to face her fears is to defeat them.

Must be true. Evalle had been scared of heights in the past but look at her now.

Opening her eyes, she glanced up, drawn to the silhouette of a lone eagle gliding across a sky on the edge of morning.

Evalle stood ready. She could only give rise to her gryphon at the rebirth of a new day.

Haloke had promised she'd soar under the sun's warmth.

Sun. That word disturbed her thoughts.

She tried to push past her mental fog. Why should she worry about the sun? It gave life to plants, animals, and birds.

Gryphons, too.

The eagle called out, drawing her gaze back to the beautiful bird. Time to concentrate on the bird. Haloke said it would lead the way.

Her toes curled over the rock ledge.

Evalle opened her arms wide, unable to contain her excitement as the eagle banked left then right before heading toward her.

CHAPTER 21

STORM'S JAGUAR RAGED AND BATTLED the unyielding wall of wind and stones pushing him back.

He could not give up.

Haloke's voice lifted to an insane level, demanding, "I call upon you, Holy People. You owe me. I gave you two sacrifices. You promised me two deaths in return. Now is the time to give me Storm's life. His for my son's. We agreed. You may have the woman as a gift."

Two deaths.

His mate would die if he didn't reach her.

That drove his battered and bleeding jaguar to rally harder. His beast lunged forward to break through the vicious wall again.

With a Herculean effort, he made it through.

His animal landed in a limp roll with legs and tail slapping the hard ground.

After being slashed and ripped, his jaguar struggled to move.

Losing Evalle would be the end of Storm and his jaguar. His animal came up on all four paws and turned to the witch.

Storm had little control of his animal in this wounded state and called up the change once more. He'd have to use his majik again to shut down Haloke before she hurt Evalle.

His jaguar held firm, not giving in.

What? Storm forced everything into changing.

Not happening.

Half-mad from surviving that bludgeoning, his jaguar turned toward Evalle.

So caught up in her homicidal pleas, Haloke failed to realize Storm's jaguar had escaped her wind attack until his cat roared.

Haloke jerked around in shock and started chanting again.

His jaguar yanked his head back to her.

Storm begged his animal to stand down and shift.

His animal roared louder, showing his fangs to the witch.

All at once, she calmed and laughed. "You can't kill me. You need me. If your beast attacks me, you'll never save Evalle." Her eyes cut to the silhouette Storm had seen as first light seeped into the eastern horizon.

Evalle hadn't moved during all the roaring and Haloke's screaming. She had to be under a spell.

Seeing through his animal's eyes, Storm finally realized why she faced away from him and toward the west. She stood on the edge of a cliff.

Haloke laughed. "I control her. You can't kill me."

His animal started for Haloke.

Storm roared at his jaguar to let him shift.

Haloke panicked. Insanity bloomed in her face. Her eyes were wild with crazy.

She started chanting furiously in Evalle's direction.

His gaze shot to their mate.

Evalle stretched her arms wide.

Storm screamed at his jaguar to stop the witch.

His massive cat dove at her, knocking the witch to the ground. He ripped her head off with a swipe of his sharp claws.

Without another thought for the seer, his jaguar lunged around and raced for Evalle. His powerful legs stretched out at preternatural speed.

Sunlight threatened to break the horizon any second.

He wouldn't get there in time for Storm to cloak her.

An eagle circled above her and swooped, flying past where she stood.

Evalle leaped off the ridge.

CHAPTER 22

EYES ON THE EAGLE GLIDING in front of her, Evalle bent her knees and leaped into the air. She opened her arms, waiting for her gryphon to break free with its huge beautiful wings.

No wings.

She couldn't hear Haloke speaking to her.

A wild roar blasted behind her.

She twisted to look over her shoulder. A black jaguar lunged off the cliff. Falling.

Storm's jaguar!

Her mind broke free of her mental fog. She realized everything at once and flipped over, screaming, *"Noooo!"*

Time turned into tiny microseconds that stretched with each drawn-out heartbeat.

Her heart thumped once. She and Storm would die unbound. She'd never find him in the afterlife.

Her heart thumped again. Red eyes glowing, Storm shifted into his human body. He yelled, *"We're bonding!"*

They were too far apart for his words or majik to reach her.

Another thump. No. No. No. She would not let him die.

Furious at the universe, Evalle bellowed, "No more! I want my gryphon back. *It is mine! Storm is mine!"* She reached deep insider her to the core where energy began to spin. The Belador power she possessed boiled.

Yes! The power that belonged to her.

Garwyli said to believe.

She called her gryphon, refusing to be told no.

Energy exploded inside her ... but no beast.

Storm turned his body into a knife shape, slicing the air faster.

She shoved her hands up to slow him with kinetics until she hit the ground. She hoped his jaguar could heal anything he broke.

Her arms twisted and yanked away in two directions.

Pain ripped through her. Her head warped and grew.

Two strong thumps. Her heart felt ten times its size. Pain stabbed her head and body.

Lights flashed through her eyes.

She moved her arms.

Her fall slowed.

A blue-green wing flapped into view.

Her gryphon! Yes!

Storm yelled, "Save yourself!"

Flapping her giant wings hard, she lurched over to look down. Ground coming too fast.

She opened her wings wide, begging for an updraft. Twisting her gryphon head, seconds stretched. Storm barreled toward her.

Wind caught her wings, shoving her upright.

That took her out from under Storm. Damn.

She wouldn't catch him.

His body would smash against the rocks below.

With one last chance, she lunged her gryphon hard. Please let Storm's body slam into her.

Either she could take the hit and save them or they'd both die.

Brown eyes now wide with realization, he yelled, "*Nooo!*"

Sorry, sweetheart. You have no vote in this. But Storm couldn't hear her thoughts.

Flipping like an out-of-control kite in a wind, her gryphon slammed against Storm before he passed her. That knocked him further out where the jagged slope dropped deeper.

She dove after his spiraling body.

Had him and the canyon floor in sight.

Extending her claws, Evalle's gryphon shuddered with strain to reach Storm.

She wouldn't make it.

Calling up all the power her gryphon could give, she tucked her wings tight. Her gryphon blasted forward.

Claws extended, she latched onto Storm's thick shoulder and opened her wings fast.

Her body yanked brutally.

Ow, ow, ow. That hurt like hell. But she forced her gryphon to keep flapping to slow their descent.

Her heart pounded. Still falling fast. Not enough time to recover.

Suddenly, majik flowed around her.

She caught the sound of Storm's chanting.

New energy surged through her. Her beast banked hard to the right twenty feet from slamming into the ground. So close dust blew up. Then her gryphon launched toward the sky.

They lifted above the cliffs.

Sunlight burst over the horizon.

Storm couldn't have cloaked them while flooding her with his majik.

Her gryphon screamed a victorious sound.

Evalle had her mate, her gryphon, her life, and a new gift. Her beast could fly in sunlight.

After gliding back and forth, her gryphon headed for the cliff Evalle had been standing on. Had she really jumped from there thinking she could fly?

So many mistakes.

Descending in a slow approach, her gryphon gently released Storm barely above the ground where her mate dropped into a roll, then came up on his feet.

Her gryphon continued flying, taking its time returning to the cliff.

She didn't care. If someone saw her, she doubted anyone would believe the story. It might make for a great photo on the cover of the rumor rags.

Flying back to Storm, her gryphon executed a graceful landing.

Storm stood with blood running down his shoulders.

The overwhelming need to feel him hit her in her middle. Her mate lived. Evalle asked for her human body again.

Running toward her, Storm shouted, *"Don't! No! Stop shifting until ... "*

It took a split second for his panic to make sense. *The sun would fry her human body!*

She didn't have his control when it came to changing. Adrenaline flooding her body dulled the ferocious pain of shifting so quickly.

She couldn't understand Storm's words.

She finished in a hunched form and lifted up as Storm caught her to him, still chanting wildly. He stopped, panted for air, and said, "Shit. The cloaking worked. I didn't know if I had enough majik left."

Good thing or she'd have died, burned to a crisp by the sun climbing higher. She'd been so caught up in the moment, so happy to feel alive after flying beneath the hot sun, she'd wanted to share that moment with her mate.

He held her so tight her bones might break.

Her gryphon would heal her.

"Thought I'd lost you forever," he breathed out in a hoarse voice.

Hugging him just as hard, she rambled through her tears. "I thought I'd watch you smash into the rocks. I never want to feel that desperate again." Desperate enough to believe? Garwyli had been right. Pulling back, she looked at Storm. She once thought there would be no joy like flying again, but seeing her mate's beautiful teak-colored face, shiny brown eyes, and black hair flying around defined true joy as nothing else could.

He pulled her close and touched her lips with his in a kiss born of fear and incredible love that would withstand all forces in this world and the next.

When his lips softened, he dropped his forehead against hers. "I don't want you out of my sight for a while. Yell at me all you want, but I'm not ready to be the bigger person and give you space any time soon."

She smiled at her man, happy for a million reasons, but mostly because she'd have more time with him. He could go caveman for a while. She could handle it. Shoot, they might have some role-playing fun back home where it would end in bed.

"Thank you," he murmured so heartfelt it brought more tears to her eyes.

"For what? I jumped off a damn cliff," she groused.

"For believing in yourself again, sweetheart. That's how you saved us. Seeing you alive and smiling ... there's no greater gift." His chest expanded with shuddering breaths.

"Are my eyes bright green again?"

"Yes, beautiful as ever."

Relieved, her hand slipped off his shoulder and slid through his blood. He still needed to heal. "I'm sorry I stabbed you with my claws, Storm."

"I'm not. My skin is already healing, and you know I can do it super fast in my jaguar form." Then he grinned. "Just like you can. Your gryphon is back, sweetheart."

"I know." She thought back to teetering on the cliff. "I remember standing there for a long time, clearing my mind of all that bothered me and waiting for an inner calm. Then I felt my body relax and thought I'd reached that peaceful moment. Haloke said I would see the eagle then I had to follow it in flight, which I thought meant my gryphon would return. I don't think that was her plan, though, was it?"

"No."

"I couldn't clear my mind of whatever she'd done with her stupid smoke, but I recall feeling as if I was in control." She frowned at him. "*I* jumped because I was under a spell, but why did *you*? Your jaguar can't fly. Wait, where is Haloke?"

"Dead. My jaguar stopped her when she tried to kill you before you jumped. At least that's how it looked to my animal and he held the control." He lowered Evalle until her feet touched the ground.

"Was she really a seer?" Evalle doubted it.

"Originally, yes, but Haloke was the person behind the supernatural killings. After her son died, she lost her mind. She left the reservation under the guise of training with a powerful seer, but evidently went somewhere and trained to become a dark witch."

"Son? Would that be a guy named Roy?"

"Yes. Did she mention him?"

"Adsila brought him up first and called the seer Mother Haloke." Evalle ran mentally over all that transpired. "Adsila brought me to Haloke. She has to know what's going on."

Storm couldn't stop touching Evalle, brushing his hand over her face and hair. "She does. Bidziil had security hunting her. They would've grabbed her as soon as they saw her on the highway, or she returned to the casino."

Evalle's head spun with that information. Furious at realizing what must have happened, she said, "Did that bitch send you off the cliff, too?"

His smile dimmed and he turned serious. Lifting a hand to catch hair flying around and push it off her face, he said, "As we fell, my jaguar and I were in agreement to reach you and see if I could save you with majik. If not, then I'd have tried to bind us any way possible so we would go together."

Tears ran down her face. She didn't care.

Now that she had no fear of killing Storm, she'd bond with him. She put to bed any other question of him dying if she did after bonding. She understood Storm's urgent need to be joined forever and felt just as strongly to stay with him.

They were partners in this life and the next.

Catching Storm's hand, she brought it to her lips and kissed his knuckles. "Bond with me."

His arm wrapped her up tighter. He whispered, "Anything for you, sweetheart."

CHAPTER 23

EVALLE HAD NEW EYES FOR the rugged landscape they passed as Storm drove them through northern Arizona.

The day had been a blur from the moment Bidziil showed up at the cliffs this morning in a Suburban. Storm took control, cloaking the vehicle, then wrapped Evalle in a blanket Bidziil produced from the cargo area.

Her poor mate had been bled dry of majik by that point. Storm climbed into the back where he pulled her into his lap, leaving Bidziil to drive them back to their villa.

His uncle had gained more knowledge about their preternatural world than he probably ever wanted.

But he'd been genuinely relieved they'd survived. Haloke's death hurt Bidziil, but he held no ill will toward Storm. He couldn't forgive the woman for what she'd done to Sonny, Imala, or them.

Evalle never carried a grudge and considered herself a forgiving person if someone made amends, but Haloke never would for the deaths. Those young men no longer had a life ahead of them once she turned them into collateral damage in her personal war of vengeance.

Every time Evalle saw Storm falling to his death, she wanted to rip Haloke to pieces.

Storm's hand reached for hers, folding their hands together and bringing Evalle back to their peaceful drive.

He asked, "What has your emotions worked up?"

"Just thinking about Haloke and Adsila. What a sick pair."

"That's an accurate description."

The seer had been cruel to Bidziil, but Storm's uncle would recover. Seeing Storm alive went a long way toward his healing.

Evalle mused, "I just can't get over how Haloke could blame Bidziil for her son's death after he'd done so much for Roy. He did all that because he'd cared about her when he was young."

Storm cocked his head. "Where'd you find that out?"

"That old blabbermouth, Yazzle, when we visited Bidziil's office today. According to Yazzle, Bidziil had been angry about Haloke marrying a non-tribe member who left her pregnant, but he still cared for her and wouldn't turn his back. That's why he took an interest in Roy."

Before the meeting with the elders and Bidziil, she and Storm had showered and crashed, promising to visit later and debrief everyone. They slept hard for six hours.

Their wild lovemaking had been one to remember for all time.

"Everyone talked too much at the same time in Bidziil's office," Storm grumbled. "My jaguar wanted out of there."

"They did, but I guess that's how that group functions," Evalle agreed. She gave Storm's hand a squeeze and received a smile she would now see again and again.

Storm reminded her, "You were telling me about talking to Yazzle."

"Oh, yes." One look at her mate and her brain drifted. "Yazzle runs off at the mouth, but seems to care for your uncle. That squirrely elder couldn't get over how Adsila had used him to get information for Haloke and to cover for her when she had to slip away under the pretense of going home sick. They dated covertly. Yazzle felt guilty for everything that happened. I told him we are only responsible for our own actions."

Having taken his sunglasses off once the sun dropped low in the sky, Storm gifted her with a brown-eyed glance that said he had a wise mate.

No, Evalle couldn't claim being wise or she'd have sorted through the mess in her head sooner. Still, she believed in the saying, "You either win or learn."

She'd won and learned. Double bonus.

From now on, she'd trust in herself and her mate.

Storm admitted he'd been lost over what happened to her in Abandinu's realm.

Emotional scars for both of them were healing.

Storm mused, "Yazzle only made the mistake of trusting someone he cared about. Haloke went searching for dark majik, fully intending to use it." He drove quietly for a mile then said,

"Adsila had an unhealthy attachment to Roy and Haloke. All three were damaged people. Bidziil said Adsila hadn't sounded the least bit remorseful. She cursed him, us, everyone for killing Roy. She gloated over her part in the deaths."

"Sounds like Roy got his self-destructive genes from his mother," Evalle noted.

"True." Storm tapped a finger on the steering wheel as if in thought. He finally said, "I've gained a whole new appreciation for my uncle and the way he works to improve life for his people. My dad would be surprised in a nice way and proud of his brother."

See? More learned, which meant another win.

Evalle had shared her mate's melancholy mood long enough. She'd lift his spirits with the truth he'd hear in her voice. "Your dad would be proud of you, too, for coming to help and preventing more young men from dying."

"I hope so," was all Storm would allow.

Her mate had begun to heal his heart, too. It had to be easier to care for his uncle than harbor anger.

Shaking his head, Storm beat his thumb on the steering wheel. "Haloke was delusional, but Adsila was just as much of a whack job."

"Evidently a brilliant one for what she did with that bird," Evalle pointed out. "Haloke had me convinced she could read the eagle's mind."

"That's only because you were under a spell. You said you started questioning Haloke when she said she could heal you."

Too little almost too late, Evalle added silently. Thinking over how they'd all been tricked, she said, "Adsila would make a dangerous spy with her ability to create an eagle as a robotic drone with a hidden camera. It took me getting closer to realize I didn't feel any life energy coming from it, but I also figured that was because my preternatural ability was gone."

"Crazy stuff," Storm muttered. "The eagle recorded you talking to it."

He'd moved his hand to touch hers without looking, as if he'd done so unconsciously.

She turned her hand over and gave him a little squeeze.

A whoosh of happiness rushed from her mate then he winked at her.

Grinning, she admitted, "Not my best moment talking to a bird."

"Anyone would to a big eagle that landed so close. You didn't do anything wrong."

"Other than admit I was a gryphon, among other things?" She lifted her eyebrows at him.

"Weren't you the one who told Yazzle he was only responsible for his actions? Give yourself a break."

"I guess." But she wouldn't stress over it. "Without Adsila supporting Haloke with intel and gaining her entrance to the homes of the two men who died, I don't think Haloke would have been as successful."

"I don't either," Storm agreed. "She would have turned into a powerful seer if she'd applied herself for the good of others. She cloaked her scent everywhere but her home. When Adsila dropped you at the hogan, the security team discovered Adsila had circled wide to find a place to park then walked to where she could operate her controller for the eagle. They found the car first, then heard her screaming, "I will kill that jaguar!""

"Not happening," Evalle said with conviction. Crazy woman.

So many things could've gone wrong, though.

Evalle unconsciously swiped a look at her unmarked skin. The lines had vanished after she shifted.

Adrianna would be smug, claiming she'd been right about the gryphon trying to break out.

Evalle couldn't argue the point.

"You okay?" Storm asked in a concerned voice.

"I'm fine. Sorry I didn't handle our talk about the lines better. I should have told you what Adrianna said and not lost my temper. I just ... panicked."

His fingers tightened slightly, letting her know he understood. "I can't say that I would have done differently in your shoes when I know you were trying to protect me. You suffered a trauma no one could understand no matter how much we thought we could. I think Garwyli was the only one who got it. He kept telling all of us to back off, that your healing would come from inside. You did exactly that when you shifted."

Evalle joked, "I'm not sure that would have happened this soon if Haloke hadn't convinced me to jump off a cliff."

Storm's hand clenched and his emotions rocked the cab.

She soothed, "Easy, baby."

He relaxed and pulled his emotions back. His level of control always amazed her. He'd admitted his jaguar had refused to return that control while battling Haloke, but Storm said his animal would not allow anyone to kill Evalle.

Stretching his shoulders, her mate said, "Hope you're ready to have me as your partner when we return home and you're ready to patrol the streets again."

"You think I'm going to complain about having you close?" She gave him a sly smile.

He must have been expecting her to complain. He did a double take, returning his attention to the road. "You usually snap at me about being able to do your Belador duty and how you can't with me hovering."

"Maybe I want to hover over *you* for a while."

He uttered a surprised, "Really?"

She now understood what he'd gone through for so long. She came clean. "I watched you almost die when I've always believed you were invincible. Oh, I worried a lot when you were on a mission, but deep inside I believed you could survive anything after getting your soul back."

His eyes warmed. "I have that because of you."

She waved that off. "We did that together, but I died a thousand times as I watched you fall. It's going to be a while before I want you out of my sight either."

Love poured in streams from Storm.

Her throat clogged with emotion.

Storm pulled her palm to his lips to kiss then laid her hand on the console again as he slowed the vehicle and took a turn off the paved road. After leaving dust in their wake on a stretch of dirt road, he found a place to park. He'd said they'd walk the final distance on the Sandal Trail that led to the Betatakin cliff dwellings where Natives had lived a thousand years ago.

A sacred place that had held significance for his father as a child.

Twilight fell across the red mountain range.

Warm wind carrying the fresh smell of the land stirred the hair she'd left to fall around her shoulders. She smoothed a hand over the beautiful pale-beige deerskin dress given her by Bidziil. He said it had belonged to his and Sani's mother.

Evalle never wore dresses, but in this moment she felt special wrapped in an outfit created with love by Storm's grandmother. Something that connected her to Storm's heritage. Like the moccasins she wore. She could never fight in them, but she wanted a pair of her own. These shoes would rock at home.

Storm would always be hot no matter what he wore, and definitely when he wore nothing, but she admired the way his tan buckskin shirt fit. It dressed up his dark jeans. Silky coal-black hair fell with a narrow braid wrapped in a tiny strand of leather hanging down the right side of his face.

After walking a ways, he led them off the trail before they reached the monument area.

"Where are we going?" She was only curious, not concerned. With both of them enjoying natural night vision again, she could see fine with yet another ten minutes until total darkness.

Had Storm brought a candle, or did he plan to majik them up a fire for light?

Singing in a deep voice drew her gaze further ahead in the direction they were walking.

A crowd of around thirty came into view. Hundreds of candles illuminated their faces.

She asked, "Who are they?"

"Bidziil said he wanted to be here and asked if he could invite others who knew my father."

Not a big gathering, but an intimate one. It had to give Storm a warm feeling to know these people remembered his father and cared enough to be here for him.

Still holding her hand, Storm guided her to where Nascha stood in spectacular Native regalia with rows of beads around his neck and an eagle feather hanging from his braid.

The three elders stood nearby, all dressed like the others in their best clothing.

Storm waited for Nascha to finish singing. When he did, Storm spoke in a smooth voice. "You honor us, old one."

"As you have honored us, son of my friend."

Tears burned the corner of Evalle's eyes, but she wouldn't allow the waterworks.

Bidziil walked over and placed a necklace of turquoise and carved beads over Storm's head then a similar one over Evalle's. His uncle paused to tell her, "You are a beautiful mate inside and out. Storm deserves you and you him. You will both be considered family from here on out. We are your people."

Damn. She couldn't stop the tears as Bidziil kissed her cheek. But one glance at Storm told her he fought his own.

His fingers clasped hers tighter as he asked, "You ready?"

"Absolutely." She drew in a deep breath and hoped she made no mistakes tonight.

Storm had gone over everything with her.

She wanted this more than ... her powers and gryphon. Those were important, but nothing compared to bonding with Storm.

She had a partner for every step of her life.

After tonight, she'd have one for all eternity.

CHAPTER 24

STORM LED EVALLE TO THEIR waiting jet, feeling a thousand times better than when he'd first landed here. He held up
two large shopping bags. "Sure you got everything?"

"Hey. If we can fly in private jets, then I can buy everyone
gifts," Evalle said, clutching another in her hand.

"You're expensive, but so worth it," he admired with a wolfish
grin.

She blushed.

Having his badass warrior do that made his day.

Storm enjoyed every minute of Evalle shopping, something
he'd never seen her do. He took her to visit the Native shops this
evening before heading to the airport. She fawned over every
handmade piece. The crafters and artists ate up her attention, then
got even more excited when Storm suggested she hadn't finished.

He pointed out she had yet to find something for Feenix.

A large shopping bag later, she moaned that she should get a
gift for Adrianna, then Tzader, Quinn and ... the list went on and
on.

He warned her to leave no one out or they'd have their feelings
hurt. He could just see her good friends, Quinn and Tzader, rolling
their eyes at that, but they would have enjoyed watching her, too.

Convincing her to buy for others had been so easy.

Did she find anything for herself? No.

That was okay. He had a gift just for her.

A different flight attendant met them at the top of the stairway.
"Mr. and Mrs. Tso, your luggage has been stowed. Once you're
comfortable, please let me know if you need anything."

"Thank you," Storm said, letting Evalle step ahead of him into
the cabin.

He handed his bags to the flight attendant as a second closed the hatch. The two found places to stow the booty.

Storm headed to the center to join Evalle. He would never tire of her joy. He could feel excitement rolling off her as they prepared to fly this time where she'd been nervous as a cat in a rocking chair factory on the flight out.

Hell, even his energy surged now that they were bonded.

They'd be linked forever.

He could sleep at night now, well, as long as she was no more than an arm's length away.

Evalle had dropped her things on the first chair she reached, then continued on to plop down on the sofa. She leaned over to take her boots off, saying, "This isn't as fast as Air Daegan, but it's much more fun and comfortable."

"What is Air Daegan, Mrs. Tso?"

Evalle's head swung up to face the flight attendant who had followed Storm as they began moving toward the runway.

Storm saved Evalle by explaining. "She's talking about a friend who transports us from time to time." He had to tell the truth in a way that covered her words, or he'd pay a price.

The woman smiled. "How nice. What can I get you?"

"We'll wait for liftoff," Storm told her. "We'll be fine until then."

She nodded and returned to the galley area where she pulled a privacy drape across the entrance, leaving them alone, just as he'd requested.

Evalle leaned forward. "I must've been zonked when we flew out. I don't remember a curtain to close off the cabin."

"They didn't use it last time," Storm replied then noticed Evalle's knee bouncing.

He put his hand on her knee and she stilled. He asked, "What's going on?"

For a moment she looked as if she wouldn't tell him, then held her hand up in a way he'd seen when she heard telepathically from someone.

When her gaze shot to him, she said, "Trey's voice blasted into my head. I think this bonding has dialed up the power of my telepathy." She grinned at her new powers.

Storm laughed. "Our energy connection might take some getting used to."

"Not. A. Problem," she answered with glee.

"Why did Trey call you?"

She said, "Oh, shoot. That's right. He said Daegan needs us in Atlanta. I told him we were on the way."

Storm hated that she'd have to return to the streets to fight preternaturals so soon, but his mate could handle it and he'd be with her.

He lowered his voice and asked, "What's the problem?"

She replied just as softly. "Some preternatural is amping up the problems with exposure to the humans."

"They were doing that when we left." Storm didn't get the new urgency. "Loki torched one of the bounty hunters in a Tribunal meeting when the guy admitted to intentionally exposing us." Before leaving today, Bidziil had told Storm how things were heating up in Atlanta and people were demanding the government find out what was going on.

Storm did his best to get Evalle packed without her seeing any videos. They had to face all that soon enough.

He figured if Daegan hadn't sent Tristan to teleport them home immediately, then they had a window of time to fly back, which Storm needed.

He had to have this moment with Evalle first.

She argued, "Yes, but we didn't know for sure the humans had enough information to believe the videos weren't hoaxes. Evidently it's getting bad and Daegan needs all of us. Trey says the dragon is running himself into the ground to handle this. Tristan told Trey he thinks Daegan is at risk if we don't circle the wagons and come up with a plan." She gave a sad sigh. "Sorry, sweetheart."

Storm ran a hand down her cheek. "Don't be. It was just a matter of time until this erupted." He asked, "Is Trey through talking to you?"

"Yep. I told him I'd let him know as soon as we made it home, but there's nothing we can do until then."

Storm relaxed. "Good. This flight is ours, a little sliver of time we don't have to share with anyone. First, back to what you were stressed about right before you heard from Trey?"

"I knew you wouldn't forget," she grumbled. After delaying another moment, she said, "Are people going to call me Mrs.

Tso?"

He hadn't expected that. He asked his carefully. "Do you want them to?"

"Not really."

"Why not?" He cringed. That came out too quick.

She shrugged self-consciously. "Because we're not married so it sounds like I'm pretending to be someone I'm not."

"You're right." He drew a breath to tell her something else. "You should never pretend to be anyone else. There is no woman like you, which is why I want you to have this." He lifted a wooden box from his pocket that had traveled with him a long time. A Dine geographic design had been inlaid on the lid with different colored wood. One of the few things he had of his father's, but the gift inside had been crafted a month ago.

Shocked, Evalle opened the box with trembling hands and stared at the silver ring with a black jaguar and green-eyed gryphon intertwined.

With night outside, he pulled her glasses off so he could see her face. "You are my mate and our bond is eternal. We live in two worlds. Ours and that of humans. I want all in both to know you are mine. Will you *marry* me, sweetheart?"

She gave him a wobbly smile. "Yes. I don't have a ring for you."

"I'll wear my father's opal, if that's okay with you."

"Of course it is. That's a great idea." She blew out a breath and said, "We should've gotten married when I had the dress Bidziil loaned me. You may never see me in one again."

"I don't care if you ever wear another. You were beautiful last night. You're beautiful in jeans, boots, and your BDU shirts. But you're stunning in nothing at all." He smoothed her hair and added, "We couldn't have our marriage ceremony in Arizona."

Her happiness dimmed. "Why not?"

"Feenix wasn't there. This will be a family event with all of our friends."

"Oh!" Evalle cried out and lunged at him. She wrapped her arms around Storm and whispered the sexy things she planned to do with her future husband when they got home.

Ever his hellion, she had another surprise coming.

Storm cupped her bottom and nipped her ear. "Have you ever heard of the Mile High Club, sweetheart?"

———•———

Thank you for reading my books. If you enjoyed this story, please help other readers find this book by posting a review.

Join my newsletter list (I NEVER share emails) at www. AuthorDiannaLove.com to be notified first about the new Belador spinoff series, **TREOIR DRAGON CHRONICLES.**

(If the link does not work, because technology sometimes gets a migraine, email assistant@authordiannalove.com with **BELADOR LIST** in the *subject line* to receive the link.)

For SIGNED & PERSONALIZED PRINT copies of Dianna's books visit *www.DiannaLoveSignedBooks.com* where you can preorder new books.

———•———

The Belador series is an ongoing story line, so you may want to read the books in order. Available in ebook/print/audio.

Book 1: Blood Trinity
Book 2: Alterant
Book 3: The Curse
Book 4: Rise Of The Gryphon
Book 5: Demon Storm
Book 6: Witchlock
Book 7: Rogue Belador
Book 8: Dragon King Of Treoir
Book 9: Belador Cosaint
Book 10: Treoir Dragon Hoard
Book 10.5: Evalle and Storm
Tristan's Escape: A Belador Novella

A NOTE ABOUT THIS STORY
FROM DIANNA

FINALLY, EVALLE AND STORM ARE bonded! I've known this story from the point I created the series. I've received so many questions about Storm's background and wanted a book specifically for these two where you would learn more about his father's side of his blood.

Thank you for allowing me to take some artistic license with things like casinos on the Navajo reservation to be able to tell this story. Any mistakes are my own and possibly are due to my need for a little flexibility to make the story work.

The uncle's casino and clan community are fictional, but I pulled information from casinos on the Navajo Reservation and other tribal lands. I've seen two sides of that story for a long time and wanted to not take one side, but to show the struggle for both sides. The Navajo, also known as the Dine people, held out longer than other tribes (it appeared they were the last major tribe to bring casinos to their land). I have the sense that waiting so long was a good thing, because that gave them the opportunity for a faster learning curve by observing other tribal casinos. I think it also allowed them to plan for how to better make it work for their people.

I often hear people outside of these reservations talk about how Native Americans are making a killing with casinos. When that off-the-cuff opinion is said to me, I share that over half the native population does not have a job and some of the many issues they face to survive and succeed. I don't judge anyone else and never form an opinion on anything without all the information. As for the Navajo and other native tribes, I feel only those living that life every day can speak to the pros and cons of any decision affecting them.

Storm has shared blood of two native groups, which allowed

me to develop someone unique.

Long before he walked into his first scene, I kept seeing his story unfold in my mind as he was forced to fight as the demon bred by his Ashaninka witch doctor mother, which conflicted with his Navajo side. He never held that against the Ashaninka, because there is good and bad among in any community. I liked the idea of a man raised to be evil, then having his soul stolen, to rise above all of that and end up being the one person who could reach Evalle, an equally damaged soul with a good heart.

They've been two of my most favorite characters to write.

Before you start sending me "Are we going to see them again?" messages, the answer is yes.

They'll continue to play prominent roles in the Belador books, as will the rest of the gang, and appear when needed in the new Treoir Dragon Chronicles series coming up next. But it was time to complete Evalle and Storm's bonding. I hope you enjoyed their journey to this point. Thank you for following the Belador series and allowing me to give life to so many stories in my head.

OTHER BOOKS BY DIANNA

If you like the Beladors, then you might enjoy Dianna's new LEAGUE OF GALLIZE SHIFTERS paranormal romance (stand alone) written with urban fantasy world building.

Gray Wolf Mate
Mating A Grizzly
Stalking His Mate

COMPLETE SLYE TEMP ROMANTIC THRILLER SERIES
Last Chance To Run
Nowhere Safe
Honeymoon To Die For
Kiss The Enemy
Deceptive Treasures
Stolen Vengeance
Fatal Promise

MICAH CAIDA YOUNG ADULT TRILOGY
Time Trap Time Return
Time Lock
The Complete Red Moon Trilogy hardback

*Signed and personalized Red Moon books available at *www. MicahCaidaSignedBooks.com* for that special reader.

(Micah Caida is the collaborative name of
New York Times Bestseller Dianna Love and
USA Today bestseller Mary Buckham)

Dianna's books can be ordered signed
and personalized from
www.DiannaLoveSignedBooks.com

AUTHOR'S BIO

NEW YORK TIMES BESTSELLER DIANNA Love once dangled over a hundred feet in the air to create unusual marketing projects for Fortune 500 companies. She now writes high-octane romantic thrillers, young adult and urban fantasy. Fans of the best-selling Belador urban fantasy series will be thrilled to know more books are coming after Dragon King of Treoir. Dianna's Slye Temp sexy romantic thriller series wrapped up with Gage and Sabrina's book–Fatal Promise–but Dianna is working on HAMR BROTHERHOOD, a new spinoff series (will include some of the Slye Temp characters). Look for her books in print, e-book and audio. On the rare occasions Dianna is out of her writing cave, she tours the country on her BMW motorcycle searching for new story locations. Dianna lives in the Atlanta, GA area with her husband, who is a motorcycle instructor, and with a tank full of unruly saltwater critters.

Visit her website at *www.AuthorDiannaLove.com* or Join her **Dianna Love Reader Community** group page on Facebook and get in on the fun!

A WORD FROM DIANNA...

NO BOOK HAPPENS WITHOUT A great supporting cast. My husband leads that list. He's always willing to do anything from cooking and driving me to locations (so I can type as he drives) for research to not calling the guys in white coats after listening to my sometimes incoherent mutterings as I walk through the house. He is my rock.

I want to give a shout out to those who have edited and beta read for me – Jodi Henley, Judy Carney, Stacey Krug, Elizabeth Neal, Sherry Arnold and Jennifer Cazares. I don't think any one person can catch everything, but these ladies have been a tremendous help with their sharp eyes.

I need to take a moment to give a special thanks to Joyce Ann McLaughlin who is often an early reader, but always my audio editor as the story is narrated. Stephen R. Thorne has done an outstanding job narrating. I found him because you, the fans, told me you loved him – you were spot on. These two make it possible for me to deliver the very best quality audio I can. I really appreciate those two, and Blackstone Audio, who distributes my Belador audiobooks.

Sending out a big hug and thanks to Candace Fox, Kimber Mirabella, Leiha Mann and Sharon Livingston Griffiths, who have been wonderfully supportive any time I need help. They're bright women who have all lead interesting lives.

Once again, Kim Killion climbed inside my head and pulled out exactly what I wanted for a cover. I love all her covers, I just love mine more. (lol) Jennifer Litteken and her team continue to perform their magic on my book formatting, always doing a great job.

Last, and definitely not least, I want to thank *you*, my readers. When I first sat down to write many years ago, I never imagined anyone would read my books. I just wanted to see if I could do it. Because of you, I'm still doing it. Much love to all of you.

Now, I'm back in the cave working on a very special spinoff of the Belador series – TREOIR DRAGON CHRONICLES.

Thank you,

Dianna

CPSIA information can be obtained
at www.ICGtesting.com
Printed in the USA
LVHW052009081019
633565LV00015B/1201/P

9 781940 651026